*Every town has stories of its past, and Havenwood Falls is no different. And when the town's residents include a variety of supernatural creatures, those historical tales often become Legends. This is but one . . .*

Three sister witches escape the Salem witch trials when the eldest casts a spell that sends their souls forward in time. Separated by unknown forces, their soul journeys place them into new lives, causing them to continually try to find one another each time.

After their second soul journey, two of the three Howe sisters end up in an unforgiving mountain range in the early 1700s, but before they can begin to search for their sister, they come face-to-face with a native tribe living in a secluded box canyon. Forced to shift their focus from their lost sibling, the girls quickly realize they've been trapped in a time loop and now must face the tribe, whose end goal remains to be seen.

When they discover that magic is being misused, the sisters put a plan into motion that will change the canyon forever, hopefully keeping others from falling into the same trap. But as their deaths loom and their next soul journey awaits, they must decide who will protect this special land and the magic of the falls once they're gone.

# LOST IN TIME

## A LEGENDS OF HAVENWOOD FALLS NOVELLA

## TISH THAWER

LEGENDS OF HAVENWOOD FALLS BOOKS

*Lost in Time* by Tish Thawer
*Dawn of the Witch Hunters* by Morgan Wylie
*Redemption's End* by Eric R. Asher
*Trapped Within a Wish* by Brynn Myers (July 2018)
*Blood and Damnation* by Belinda Boring (August 2018)

More books releasing on a monthly basis

Also try the signature New Adult/Adult series, Havenwood Falls, and the YA series, Havenwood Falls High

Stay up to date at www.HavenwoodFalls.com

Subscribe to our reader group and receive free stories and more!

## ALSO BY TISH THAWER

### The Rose Trilogy:

*Scent of a White Rose (Book #1)*

*Roses & Thorns (Book #1.5)*

*Blood of a Red Rose (Book #2)*

*Death of a Black Rose (Book #3)*

### The Women of Purgatory Trilogy:

*Raven's Breath (Book #1)*

*Dark Abigail (Book #2)*

### The Witches of BlackBrook Series:

*The Witches of BlackBrook (Book #1)*

*The Daughters of Maine (Book #2)*

### The Ovialell Series:

*Aradia Awakens (Book #1)*

*Dark Seeds (Book #1.5 – A short-story novella)*

*Prophecy's Child (An Ovialell Short Story)*

*The Rise of Rae (An Ovialell Short Story)*

*Shay and the Box of Nye (An Ovialell Short Story)*

*Behind the Veil (An Ovialell Omnibus)*

## Additional Works

*Magical Bullet Journal & Planner*

*Handler*

*Fairy Tale Confessions*

*Dance With Me (A Short Story*

*originally featured in Fairy Tale Confessions)*

*Losing It: A Collection of V-Cards*

*Christmas Lites II*

"Return us to our journey's end, find our sister, lost again. Use the bond that unites the three, as we will it, so mote it be."

— Tish Thawer

# PROLOGUE

# $\mathcal{I}$PSWICH, MASSACHUSETTS – 1693

*OUR SOUL JOURNEYS begin - Kara Howe*

### KARA

Kenna and I held tightly to Jeremiah as we watched Karina being pulled through the crowd. She was whipped around and tied to the stake, her long auburn hair lashing her face as she looked out over a sea of hateful faces who would love nothing more than to see her burn. With no solid proof, Governor Danforth announced her conviction and cast a torch at her feet. Flames rose, flickering closer and closer to her shoes and blackening the bottom of her cotton petticoat and apron as she struggled against the ropes holding her in place.

*Karina, please. Use your magic to escape.* Using our magical bond, I sent my deepest wish into Karina's mind as tears streaked down my face. Karina's only reply: a simple, peace-filled smile and the building of magic in the air.

My auburn hair—a perfect match to both my sisters'—fell forward from beneath my white coif and covered my freckled face. Bowing my head, I listened to Karina's inner plea to the goddess. Kenna, Jeremiah, and I all closed our eyes and surrendered to Karina's spell pulling our souls forward through time. Surrounded by wind and fire, we escaped this unbearable life of wrongful convictions as our astral bodies spun wildly into the starry night. Sparking against one another, we recognized each other's magic and knew Karina had just saved us all.

Opening my eyes, I took in the unfamiliar space but quickly understood how the soul journeys now worked. Solidified into my new lifetime, information flowed into my mind, filling in details of the person I would now be living as. I looked around the room and saw two others—a man and a younger woman—standing directly across from me. Thankfully, I was fully cognizant that despite their outward appearance, it was actually Jeremiah and Kenna who remained with me. I quickly glanced around at the rest of the room, and my heart clenched as I realized, however, Karina was not.

# CHAPTER 1

 PEN TERRITORY—June 1703

*OUR SECOND SOUL JOURNEY. Karina was not found in our previous lifetime. After her initial spell, we were all pulled to Salem a few years in the future, but were unable to locate her there. It took months of using our magic to even pinpoint her, but shortly after that, her signature was permanently lost. She had died and jumped again, and we were not far behind. Hopefully this time, we will have better luck. ~ Kara Howe*

KARA

I woke within the safety of what appeared to be a large covered wagon. A thick, dingy canvas stretched tight over hickory bows flexed above my head. I sat up, fully entrenched in my newest lifetime, and rubbed my eyes as the memory dump that

3

accompanied this soul journey quickly informed me that Kenna and I were the daughters of a fur trader—Jeremiah.

"Girls, are you all right?" Jeremiah called from the other side of the wagon.

"Yes. I'm all right," I replied, then looked to my little sister, who now wore the face of a young Spanish beauty. She had dark almond-shaped eyes and a cascade of dark flowing hair. "Kenna, are you well?"

"Yes, I am fine." Kenna sat up from beneath a bundle of covers made of skins and furs and adjusted her heavy coat and the raccoon-tail hat that sat upon her head. "But what in the world am I wearing?"

She twisted the end of her hair around her finger and stared down at her clothes, clearly distraught over the current fashions.

Jeremiah, now a Spanish fur trader named Lorenzo Vargas, sat up and adjusted the suspenders under his thick wool coat, then tugged at his newly acquired beard.

"It seems I'm a fur trader, and you two are my twin girls," he explained, confirming the answers I had already received.

Pausing for only a moment as more information filtered in, I quickly continued, "It's late spring, and we are in the open territory of a massive mountain range that has recently been claimed by Juan de Ulibarri of the Spanish conquistadors."

"Are we in danger?" Kenna's head snapped up—the curl of dark hair still wrapped around her index finger—and addressed the one thing that remained a constant pull upon her soul: our family's safety.

"No. We are safe," I confirmed, as the last filaments of information seeped into my consciousness. "Apparently, our family is one of the 'approved' traders still allowed into the villages."

"Excellent. At least that is one less concern." Kenna squared her shoulders and released the lock of hair. Uncinching the ties that let in a blast of frigid mountain air, she moved to exit the back of the wagon. "You two rest while I scan the area and put our protection spells in place. We will begin our search for Karina in the morning."

She shivered, pulling down her fur cap, and then stepped out into the pitch-black night.

Jeremiah and I exchanged nods, knowing we were in good hands, then settled back into the warmth of our own fur coverings.

## CHIEF AQUAKAWWA

Scents of sage, mugwort, and a hint of copal wafted from the fire as I sat with my shaman in the center of our village. Mountains surrounded us on all sides, rising into the horizon and backlit against a starlit sky.

"A change has arrived," my shaman said in our native tongue. His weathered face and gray-tinged braids hung low as he focused intently on the smoke rising from the burning embers.

I turned and glanced around the village, but found nothing out of place. "The family teepees remain tightly arranged within the box canyon from winter. I see no change," I replied.

"You will. When the trader and his family come from the west, do not send them away." The shaman rose from the log he had been seated upon and turned to leave, stopping with just one last thing to say. "Do this, and our tribe will no longer face the threat of war, be it from the Comanche or the white man."

The elder shuffled off, and when he was no longer in view, I turned back to the fire and cupped the smoke in my hands, inhaling deeply. A haze washed over me, and I closed my eyes, allowing myself to become lost in thought as the history of our tribe played out in within my mind.

Peace for my people had always been a struggle in the changing landscape around us. Our lineage came from the larger Ute population that occupied much of the extended territory nearby, but our smaller offshoot tribe now maintained our home in the box canyon we had found during one of our southern hunting expeditions.

"There is something special about this land," my shaman had said at the time, and he was right. Rugged mountains boxed us in, and a great waterfall fed into the ponds and rivers below, providing life-sustaining resources and seclusion from the outside world—until recently.

Invading tribes threatened from the east, and the rapid movements of the Spaniards heading north in recent years had forced me to choose whether to relocate with the majority of the Ute people, or to stay behind and defend our village alone.

I made the decision quickly. Ever since, we had defended our traditional way of life in the quiet solace of this canyon and would continue to protect ourselves and the joy we had found within this special place.

I opened my eyes and sat quietly, watching the flames dance upon the air, and thought about what my shaman had said. If his vision came to pass, we would face a beautiful future no longer threatened by war. I rose from the log and looked upon the teepees scattered throughout the village, my focus settling on that of my own family dwelling. I hoped this trader and *his* family would be able to find us soon.

# CHAPTER 2

KARA

*I* woke, bouncing roughly to and fro as the wagon lurched
forward. Jeremiah must have risen before either of us
girls and set off on the trail this trader had been traveling over for
the last few weeks. I sat up and rubbed my head, foreign dark hair
cascading over my shoulders. It would take some time to get used to
not seeing the red locks my sisters and I normally shared. Our
names in this lifetime were Lorenzo, Catalina, and Clara Vargas, the
latter being myself. As twins, Kenna and I looked exactly the
same—tan skin, brown eyes, long black hair, and in our early
twenties with curvier figures than either of us were used to. We
would continue in this lifetime living as the Vargas family with all
their knowledge and memories, but it was through the magic of our
soul journeys that we were now in control and cognizant
contributors to it all.

Pushing from beneath the blankets, I climbed through the front opening to join Jeremiah on the loosely fashioned hardwood bench that sat in front of the tarp.

"Wow!" I gasped. Two large oxen, strapped and reined, strained to pull the wagon across the rough terrain. "That was unexpected."

Jeremiah huffed out a laugh. "Yes, oxen are far more capable of pulling the weight of a wagon this size and all its contents than horses would be. At least for our purposes."

"What is our purpose here? Do you know of the trader's destination yet?" I asked.

"Yes. It seems he was heading toward a secluded canyon where trade with the local Indian chief has already been approved. Though," Jeremiah scratched his beard, "he's never dealt with them before and seems a bit nervous about it."

"Well, from the information our soul journey has provided, I think that is a normal reaction for these parts in this particular time. Do you think we will be able to start looking for Karina soon?" I prompted, anxious again to start the search for our lost sister.

"Yes. Once we are safe within the village, we will finalize our business and then begin our search for Karina on the way back out. Spring is upon us, but this high up in the mountains, the temperatures still drop below freezing at night, which will make the pass we are meant to take a treacherous mess. We will need to be in and out as quickly as possible."

I nodded in understanding and continued to bounce along in my seat as the sun rose over the distant mountains. The landscape here was wild and untamed compared to our previous locale of Salem, Massachusetts, but it was shockingly beautiful. Evergreens surrounded us, glistening with a coat of frost in the late spring morning, while cragged mountains and snow-covered peaks reached far into the bright blue sky. I blew out a breath and squealed at the tiny plumes of frozen air that escaped past my lips.

"Damn, it's cold," Kenna muttered in lieu of a morning

greeting as she squeezed her way between us on the plank seat.

"That it is, little sister. Shall we do something about it?" I lifted my brows as magic played in my eyes.

Jeremiah reached across and grabbed my wrist. "No. Do not use magic out here in the open. The trials of our time may not have been heard of here, and we need to keep it that way. I will not risk exposing ourselves in an unfamiliar land."

I looked at Kenna, who had begun to twirl her hair again, and nodded at them both.

"You are right, of course." I patted Jeremiah's hand with my free one.

Kenna scooted closer, sliding under the fur that was draped across my legs, adding to our shared warmth. "If we are not going to practice magic out in the open, then how are we going to search for Karina? The last time, it took a lot of magic performed under the moon to even find a trace of her location," she asked.

"Yes, Kenna, I am aware of that too," Jeremiah replied in a smooth, even tone. "But like I have explained to Kara, we will finish our business with the Indian chief and be on our way as quickly as possible. Once we are back down the pass, it is my hope that we can make camp for the summer in a secluded area where we can cast our spells without reprisal. But, until I know where that might be, we need to keep up appearances. Understand?"

"Certainly." Kenna dipped her chin, giving Jeremiah a clipped nod as she continued to spin the thick strand of her hair.

We rode together in silence for another half mile or so before Kenna spoke again. "Speaking of appearances, I think this is the first time I have ever seen you with a full beard."

She winked at Jeremiah, a wide smile spreading across her face. Jeremiah shifted in his seat, the apples of his cheeks flushing a light red.

"Yes, it is going to take some getting used to for me as well." He gave it another scratch. "At least I have some built-in fur to help keep me warm," he teased, clearly happy his reprimand had not dampened Kenna's spirits.

Kenna and Jeremiah laughed, and I giggled at the sound, grateful that Karina's original spell had saved us all and started us on our continual soul journeys. Despite her absence—and the multiple lives we would be forced to live while continuing our search for her—at least we three would always be together.

With my heart a little lighter, I continued to make observations as the sights around me developed under the sun's morning rays. A thick layer of pine needles and dark leaves covered the forest floor beneath the evergreens, while chirping chipmunks raced through their limbs above. However, after another two hours of bouncing along the rough path and taking in the breathtaking views, it was Kenna's stomach that captured my attention.

"Goodness gracious, was that your stomach that just growled?" I whipped my head in her direction.

"Yes. I'm so sorry. Clearly, working our protections last night has sapped my energy and left me completely famished." She turned to Jeremiah. "If we can stop soon, I can prepare us something to eat. I believe I saw a small box-stove and some supplies in the back corner of the wagon."

"Wonderful. Let me get past this next bend, and I will look for a place to stop."

Kenna and I shifted our weight and climbed back through the canvas and into the rear of the wagon as Jeremiah continued to work the handbrake, guiding the oxen through the muddy terrain. After one final turn around a tight curve in the ascending trail, Jeremiah yanked hard on the reins, bringing us to a sudden stop. Pots and pans clattered around us, and we both yelped at the abruptness.

"What in the world are you trying to do, kill . . ." My words trailed off as I peeked my head back out the front of the wagon and found our path blocked by savages.

# CHAPTER 3

CHIEF AQUAKAWWA

The crunching of dirt and rocks reached my ears as the clatter of a wagon approached. I looked to my shaman and received a confirming nod, signaling these were the traders we had been waiting for. I motioned to my tribesmen and we mounted our horses. The beads and feathers in the manes of our fierce and noble creatures drifted silently on the wind as we rode forward to intercept our guests. My anticipation reached its peak as iron-rimmed wheels ground their way around the last bend in the trail.

I gave a whistle and then led my men to the entrance of the canyon, quickly blocking the wagon's path. The male had a full beard and fine clothes, but it was the dark-headed woman who had emerged from the wagon that captured my attention.

"Maiku." I lifted my hand in welcome, curious if she would understand our native tongue.

She leaned toward the man I assumed to be her father and whispered in his ear, then returned my greeting fluently. "Hello. We are the Vargas family and were sent with approval to trade with your tribe."

I smiled widely, pleased to know they had studied our native language in preparation for their trip. It was a sign of great respect. "I am Chief Aquakawwa of the Ute people. We have been expecting you. Please follow me."

I motioned my men ahead, then led the family to the northernmost point in the village, where my shaman had already set up a teepee and a hitching post for their animals. The skins for the dwelling had come from our winter stores, but my shaman had assured me it would be for a "grand and wonderful cause."

The man climbed down from his perch and tied up the oxen, releasing them from the wagon's tongue, while the girl returned to the back of the wagon, disappearing from my sight.

Still sitting astride my war-painted horse, I provided the man with instructions. "Get settled, then come to the main dwelling in the center of our village as the sun begins to set. All here are aware of your visit, and I assure your safety. You are my welcomed guests."

The man stood still as my men and I rode off in a flurry of flying dirt and pounding hooves.

KARA

As soon as the natives were out of sight, Jeremiah motioned for us to join him. Pulling back the flap of the teepee, I walked inside and gasped.

"Look at all of this!" Turning in circles, I took in the beautifully dyed clothing and moccasins laid out across handmade quilts. There were also coiled containers sealed with pitch for water storage, and weapons made of stone and wood, including bows and arrows, flint knives, arrow heads, and throwing sticks, all scattered around our new lodging. Digging sticks, weed beaters, tools, and more baskets, plus metates and manos for food preparation, lined one whole area, as if we'd be expected to stay for the spring harvest. "It is all so beautiful."

"Yes, it is. The tribeswomen are highly skilled, and their goods are very sought after. It is the reason we are here," Jeremiah explained, thanks to Lorenzo's knowledge.

Kenna ran her hand over a beaded dress lying on one of the beds, then frowned. "Are we supposed to put these on?"

Jeremiah shrugged. "The chief didn't specify, but I think it would be a show of respect if we did. But first, let us gather our supplies and fix a bite to eat while we wait for tonight's gathering."

I nodded in agreement, then led Kenna outside, filling our afternoon with the menial chores of emptying the wagon, cooking lunch, cleaning, and organizing our supplies. Once done, we each took turns behind the small fur-draped partition, donning our new attire, then waited outside for Jeremiah to do the same.

"All set." Jeremiah emerged from the teepee in a pair of dyed pants, a matching beaded vest, and a heavy fur draping slung over his shoulders which would help fight the dropping temperature at night. "The chief said to make our way to the main dwelling." He gestured to the worn footpath in front of us, then took the lead, pounding softly ahead in his fur-lined moccasins.

"I hope they have prepared some sort of meal, because I am *still* starving." Kenna rubbed her stomach, trying to inject some playfulness into her words.

"I'm sure they have. I smell some sort of roasted meat coming from up ahead," I replied, pointing toward our destination.

Kenna reached for a strand of hair and closed her eyes, twisting it around her finger as she inhaled deeply. "Oh, thank goodness. I wonder what else they have planned?"

Drums sounded at that exact moment, bringing an ominous end to our short walk. Jeremiah pulled back the flap of the main dwelling, and the pounding beat intensified, rattling our chests as we walked inside the oversized teepee. Smoke drifted from a fire pit in the center, while members of the tribe—fully dressed in elaborate headdresses and face paint—sat around the perimeter of the gathering. Chief Aquakawwa stood, and the drums fell silent.

"Welcome, friends. Please sit." He pointed to the blanket-covered log closest to the fire and waited for us to take our seats. "We welcome you into our village and celebrate with the Ute Bear Dance. This celebration traditionally marks the *beginning* of spring, but tonight we perform it in honor of you and your timely arrival." The drums picked up again and dancers moved into formation.

Shuffling feet wove intricate patterns into the dirt floor as the natives chanted and moved to the beat. Jeremiah and Kenna sat quietly, enjoying the show. I, however, found the chief and the older man whispering in the corner far more interesting.

A small bowl, filled with herbs and fragments of things I could not see, popped and hissed under the smoke of his long pipe. The elder continued to blow on the ingredients until they burst into flames, their smoke mixing with the main fire's as it spiraled up and out through the teepee's vaulted opening. Magic tingled along my skin, and I squinted, trying to read the words forming on the elder's lips. Unfortunately, from this distance, all remained unclear. At the song's crescendo, the dancers released a shout and gave a final stomp, standing tall and effectively blocking my view until the chief rose and dismissed them back to their seats.

"Spring is a time of awakening and rejuvenation. As the bear emerges from his long winter's nap, we too shall spend the season re-embracing our customs, holding tight to tribal traditions in preparation for the battle ahead." The chief opened his arms wide, motioning to the entire room, which sent the fringe hanging down from the sleeves of his shirt swinging wildly back and forth. "The constant struggle against Mother Nature's turning seasons is not the only thing we must prepare for; other forces still threaten to change our way of life."

Jeremiah, Kenna, and I all shifted uncomfortably when the chief's gaze fell upon us.

"Our new visitors are the only traders allowed within this village, and with them comes a chance for us to secure our place in the future as this land continues to change. But make no mistake, our traditions will stand, and tonight, we will begin this successful union with the customary exchanging of gifts." The chief motioned for Jeremiah to rise.

Jeremiah nervously looked back at Kenna and me, and then stood. Thankfully, my sister was quick in preparing a protection spell that she sent to us both—just in case things went askew.

"Tonight, in celebration of the upcoming Strawberry Moon, we give thanks to the protective spirits of the land. As we make this exchange, know your gift will be offered as payment to the spirits, so that they may protect and grant us prosperity in the upcoming harvests." Chief Aquakawwa reached behind him then presented Jeremiah with a stack of thick furs and skins.

Jeremiah bowed in acceptance and handed them off to Kenna, who had already cast another spell to conjure up a suitable gift in exchange. Taking the chief's offering, she handed Jeremiah a burlap-wrapped jar, its lid tied tightly with twine.

"Please accept this gift of our healing salve. It will soothe and heal any injury that may befall you," Jeremiah repeated the words that Kenna had obviously spoken into his mind.

Chief Aquakawwa took the jar and nodded, signaling the exchange was a fitting one. "The spirits are appeased. Let us eat."

A dull roar filled the teepee as the women of the tribe brought forth the meal they had prepared. Steaming bowls of meat, corn, and wild onions were presented to the chief and shaman first, then to Jeremiah and us girls. Wild raspberry, gooseberry, and what I thought to be buffalo-berry had been gathered and could be eaten raw but had also been mashed and strained to serve as our drink. Everything was fresh and delicious, though different from what we were used to. Thankfully, the Vargas family were familiar with the native fare, and their memories continued to serve as the perfect bridge between our cultural differences. This was the beauty of Karina's original spell, which allowed us to transition smoothly into each new lifetime we would have to live.

I ate in silence, enjoying the food, but kept a watchful eye on the shaman throughout the meal. After the grumblings of our stomachs were curbed, the chief announced the celebration's end, and all began to return to their homes—all except the shaman. I rose slowly from my seat and watched as he continued to mutter and fiddle with the bowl of ingredients in his lap. The chief must have noticed my hesitation, because he stepped in front of me and held out his arm, pointing to the main exit, his fringe swinging wildly again.

I smiled and left with my family, my stomach roiling as it filled with questions and concerns.

# CHAPTER 4

KARA

$\mathcal{C}$hief Aquakawwa followed us out, escorting us all the way back to our teepee.

"Thank you again for your gift. A healing salve will be most useful to my tribe. As for our official trade negotiations, they are set to take place in two days' time." The chief bowed his head, his long black braids falling forward as he stared at the ground, then turned to leave without another word.

Once inside, Kenna and I took turns discarding our heavy dresses, changing instead into the lightweight nightclothes the Vargas girls were used to wearing. Though with the temperatures still dropping at night, a fur draping would be required over our cotton petticoats to fight against the bone-numbing chill in the air.

"That was . . . interesting," Kenna said as she climbed into the warmth of her cot.

"Yes, I agree," I replied, finding my way under the blankets as Jeremiah stoked the fire in the center of the room. "Did you notice the shaman chanting during their dance? I hope I wasn't the only one who felt something was off."

"No, I didn't notice. But then again, I was concentrating on the chief," Jeremiah replied. "He seems eager to welcome us and accept our trade, but there was something intense in the way he discusses their history and traditions."

"I agree," I continued. "We need to be careful here. The rise of magic was distinct during their dance, and I think the shaman was attempting to cast some sort of spell."

"Were you able to identify what the root of it was?" Kenna asked.

I shook my head, still getting used to her Latin features and habits, instead of her usual light-skinned, red-haired self. "No. I could not see his ingredients or hear the chant he seemed to be whispering. Either way, I think tomorrow we should try to get back into that tent."

Kenna nodded and Jeremiah agreed, finally crawling into his own bed and drawing the fur coverings up to his neck.

KARA

Pots and pans rattled in the wagon as we bounced along the rough terrain in the foreign mountain-scape our soul journey had brought us to. Jeremiah must have woken before either of us girls and . . .

"Ouch!" I grabbed my head, rubbing small circles against the sharp pain that shot through my temples. With the pressure slightly relieved, I climbed through the front opening and joined Jeremiah on the wooden bench. "Oh my! How unexpected," I exclaimed, shaking my head against the lingering sting.

"Yes, oxen are far more capable of pulling the weight of a wagon this size . . ." Jeremiah paused and ran a hand over the back of his neck.

I looked to the sky, taking in the scenery as the morning rays lit up the snow-covered peaks.

"Have we been here before?" I asked, frustrated at the strange nagging feeling in my head.

"No. I do not think so." Jeremiah continued to rub the back of his neck. "It seems we are heading toward a secluded canyon, where trade with the local Indian chief has already been approved."

Another sunburst of pain shot through my temples. I leaned back against the canvas of the wagon and took a deep breath. The wild landscape surrounding us was breathtaking. I concentrated on the tops of the evergreens as they reached far into the sky, glistening with a coat of frost in the late spring morning.

"Damn, it's cold." Kenna squeezed her way out the opening, dragging with her a heavy fur, and flopped between us on the board.

"That it is, little sister." I lifted the edge of the blanket and scooted over, making room as she draped it across our legs.

"Speaking of appearances . . ." Kenna started—though no one had been speaking of anything of the sort. She smiled and pointed at Jeremiah's beard.

Jeremiah yanked at the scruff on his chin. "Yes. I know. It will definitely take some getting used to . . ."

"But at least you have some built-in fur to help keep you warm," Kenna finished for him.

Jeremiah shook his head, rubbing his neck again. "How did you know I was going to say those exact words?"

"I . . . do not know," Kenna gasped. Claiming a piece of her hair between her fingers, she looked around nervously and continued to make observations at the sights around us. "I wonder why the Vargas family never came this far south before?"

19

I looked between the two, confused and feeling severely off-kilter myself.

Jeremiah tilted his head up to the sky and replied, "I honestly don't think *any* outsiders have ventured this far into the region before."

We all fell silent and listened as the sounds of the forest continued to wake around us—the crunch of snow under unknown hooves, the chattering of animals racing through the trees, and songs from the wind whipping between the boughs overhead. It was all so unbelievably peaceful—if one could block out the distracting clatter of the wagon.

I snapped my head toward Kenna as a loud grumble sounded from her direction.

"Goodness gracious, was that your stomach that just growled?" I asked.

"Yes. I'm sorry. Clearly . . ." She paused, pinching the bridge of her nose. "I think I am in need of a good breakfast. If we can stop, I can whip us up something to eat. I think there are some supplies in the back of the wagon."

"Let me get past this next bend, and I will look for a place to pull off," Jeremiah quickly replied.

I shifted my weight and followed Kenna back into the wagon as Jeremiah worked the handbrake to guide the oxen through the muddy terrain. Suddenly, he must have yanked hard on the reins, because pots and pans rattled around us as we came to a sudden stop.

"What in the world . . ." My words trailed off as I peeked back out the front of the wagon and found our path blocked by savages.

# CHAPTER 5

KARA

"*M*aiku!" An Indian astride a large painted horse raised his hand and addressed me directly in his native tongue.

I leaned toward Jeremiah and whispered, "Give me just a moment," then I cast a quick language spell that would encompass us all:

*"Language yours, language mine, bridge the gap and intertwine.*
*Understood, shall we be, as I will it, so mote it be."*

With the spell in place, I understood and returned the man's greeting. "Hello. We are the Vargas family and were sent with approval to trade with your tribe."

"I am Chief Aquakawwa. We have been expecting you. Please follow me."

The chief motioned his men ahead, then led us to the

northernmost point in the village, where a beautifully painted teepee had already been erected. There was also a hitching post for our oxen and from the looks of the smoke rising out the top of the structure, a fire already built within.

Jeremiah climbed from his perch and tied up our animals, releasing them from the wagon's tongue while Kenna and I remained hidden in the back.

Still astride his horse, the chief dismissed his men and provided Jeremiah with instructions. "Get settled, then come to the main dwelling in the center of our village once the sun begins to set. All here are aware of your visit, and I can assure your safety. You are my welcomed guests."

I peeked through the front opening and saw Jeremiah nod in understanding with a clenched jaw. He stood still with his arms crossed over his chest as the chief and his men rode off. Once they were out of sight, he waved us down.

Kenna and I climbed from the wagon and quickly entered the teepee. I pulled back the flap and walked inside, gasping as another sharp pain shot through my head. Rubbing my temples, I stood awestruck, taken aback by the scene.

"Look at all of these beautiful wares."

"Indeed." Jeremiah frowned as he circled the room. "The tribeswomen are highly skilled . . ." His words trailed off, and he ran a hand through his hair, stopping to rub at the back of his neck again.

"Are we supposed to put these on?" Kenna asked, pointing to a beaded dress laid out across a cot.

"The chief did not specify, but I think it would be a show of respect if we did." Jeremiah shrugged. "But first, let us gather our supplies and fix a bite to eat while we wait for tonight's gathering."

Agreeing, Kenna and I set ourselves to task. We unloaded the wagon, sorted and cleaned our supplies, then prepared a small lunch before taking turns behind the fur-draped partition to don our new attire.

"All set." Jeremiah emerged from the teepee in a pair of dyed pants, a matching beaded vest, and a thick fur slung over his shoulders. "The chief said to make our way to the main dwelling." He gestured to the worn footpath in front of us, taking the lead but stumbling slightly.

"Are you okay?" Kenna asked, grabbing him by the elbow.

"Yes. I'm fine, but obviously, this trip has taken a toll. Hopefully, they will have prepared some sort of meal, because I think a little more nourishment would do us all some good."

I looked back at Kenna with my brows drawn tight, not wanting to alert Jeremiah to my concern as we continued on.

"I'm sure they have." Kenna sniffed the air. "I smell some sort of roasted meat coming from that direction."

Jeremiah drew in a deep breath and closed his eyes. "Smells good. I wonder what else they have planned?"

Drums sounded at that exact moment, bringing an ominous end to our short walk. The pounding beat grew in intensity as Jeremiah pulled back the flap of the oversized teepee. Smoke drifted from a fire pit in the center, while members of the tribe—fully dressed in elaborate headdresses and face paint—sat around the perimeter of the gathering. Chief Aquakawwa stood, and the drums fell silent.

"Welcome, friends. Please sit."

Jeremiah, Kenna, and I walked forward and took seats upon the blanket-covered log closest to the fire. I reached for Kenna, who had dropped her head and pinched the bridge of her nose as soon as she was seated.

"Are *you* all right?" I whispered.

She closed her eyes and shook her head but did not respond as the chief began to speak.

"Tonight, we welcome you into our village and celebrate your arrival with the Ute Bear Dance. This celebration traditionally marks the *beginning* of spring, but today we perform it to honor you and your timely arrival." The drums picked up again and dancers moved into formation.

Kenna lifted her head, seemingly recovered, and sat quietly next to Jeremiah, twirling her hair as they enjoyed the show. I, however, was drawn to the chief and the older man whispering in the corner. Herbs popped and hissed in a small bowl as the elder blew smoke over it from his long pipe. The dancers' movements faded into my periphery as I stared intently at the ingredients until they burst into flames. Pain shot through my head and magic crawled across my skin. Squinting against the throb in my temples, I focused on the shaman again, trying to make out the words forming on his lips. Unfortunately, from this distance, I simply could not. At the song's crescendo, the dancers released a shout and gave a final stomp, standing tall and effectively blocking my view until the chief rose and dismissed them back to their seats.

"Spring is a time of awakening and rejuvenation. As the bear emerges from his long winter's nap, we too shall spend the season re-embracing our customs and . . ."

"AHHH!"

Chief Aquakawwa's words petered off as I grabbed my head and screamed.

KARA

I woke to the sounds of arguing outside of our teepee.

"What is happening to her? What did your shaman do?"

Jeremiah's huff was distinct and familiar, while Chief Aquakawwa's voice remained low, yet audible.

"I assure you, nothing is amiss. The herbs our shaman uses are nothing out of the ordinary and are used to cleanse and purify our ritual space. Nothing more. I am sure your daughter is just worn out from her long journey. Please rest, and we can discuss more in the morning."

I remained quiet and listened to the chief shuffle away, but sat up when Kenna and Jeremiah reentered through the thick flap covering the door.

"What happened?" I asked.

"You screamed, then lost consciousness during the welcome celebration," Jeremiah explained.

"Oh my goodness! Did I offend the chief?"

"No. That was *all* me," Kenna snapped, kicking her moccasins into the corner. Silence hung in the air as she disappeared behind the changing screen, reemerging in her nightclothes and claiming a seat at the end of my bed. "Do you remember anything about what happened?"

I lay back down, massaging my temples as I thought back. "I remember arriving, cleaning out the wagon, having lunch, organizing the supplies here in the teepee . . ." I paused, looking at the tools and weapons against the far wall. "Then walking to the gathering, the dance starting, and . . ."

"And . . . ?" Kenna prompted, reaching for a thick swath of her hair.

"And . . . magic!"

"Yes! I knew it." Kenna bounced from the cot and walked to where the baskets and bowls were stacked between two support beams. "Look at these. Do you not remember them being clean and new when we arrived?" She held them out for Jeremiah and me to see. Frayed threads hung from the baskets, and scrapes from

25

vigorous cleaning marred the bowls, inside and out. "How did they become like this in a matter of *hours?*"

I gasped. "What are you saying?"

"I am saying, something is not right here, and we need to be careful. I asked the chief to explain what the shaman was chanting during the dance, and well . . . as you may have heard, everything is supposedly *fine* and nothing is *amiss.*" Kenna walked to her own cot and crawled beneath the covers, frantically spinning a curl between her fingers. "But I do not believe him. We need to remain alert."

# CHAPTER 6

KARA

*P*ots and pans rattled around me as I woke within the covered wagon. Jeremiah must have risen before either of us girls and set off on the trail this trader had been traveling over for the last few weeks. We were the Vargas family in this lifetime, and . . .

"Ahhhh!" A scream tore from Jeremiah at the front of the wagon.

I jumped up and pushed out the opening, scrambling to claim the reins and yanking the oxen to a stop as Kenna burst through the tarp with a small pistol in hand. "What is wrong?"

Jeremiah fisted his hair and began rocking back and forth.

"I do not know." I yanked the handbrake into place. "Help me get him inside so I can scan him," I instructed.

Kenna placed her hands under Jeremiah's shoulders and pulled, while I lifted his legs and pushed him back into the safety of the wagon bed.

*"God and Goddess hear my plea, through your vision let me see.
Reveal to us the wrongness here, allowing me to cure those dear."*

Visions of disjointed scenes filled my head: Indian celebrations, meals being shared, the three of us working the fields in a summer that had yet to come, friends becoming family through native customs, all set against the wild landscape in a canyon surrounded by mountains on all sides. Some things seemed the same, while others were slightly different, yet all were somehow looped together.

I tried to focus on the images, pinpointing their origin, and suddenly my magic wavered, but not before I caught sight of one last thing . . . a shaman burying an item under three beds in a grand teepee.

"Oh no!" I pulled back my hands, severing the connection.

"What is it? What is wrong with him?" Kenna pleaded, dabbing his forehead with a damp towel.

"There is nothing wrong with him . . . *yet.*"

"What on earth do you speak of? Look at him!"

"What I am saying is, whatever is affecting him has not happened yet . . . *or* has already happened before. I do not understand it all, but I think time is being manipulated around us." Kenna stared at me wide-eyed as I continued to explain. "What is clear, however, is that something happened—or *happens*—once we arrive in the Indian village. I believe it is the catalyst for this entire situation."

"Should we rather not go?" Kenna posed the obvious question.

I shrugged, unsure. "I do not know. Whatever this time spell is, it has already been cast upon us, so at this point, I am not sure it would even matter."

"Then, how exactly do we figure that out?" She reached for the end of her thick raven hair.

I thought for a moment, recalling what I had seen. "Well, we could either continue to the village with the awareness we now possess and try to find the objects I saw in my vision, *or* we could stay here and not arrive today as planned, to see if that changes anything. Unfortunately, if I'm right, that means everything may just start over again tomorrow, leaving us to hopefully figure it out once more." I took the rag from Kenna's hand and dabbed Jeremiah's brow. "Personally, I say we continue on as planned, use this knowledge to discover the root of the spell, and put a stop to it as soon as possible."

Kenna nodded, pushing back to sit against the canvas of the far wall. "I agree. Once Jeremiah is well, let us continue on as though nothing has changed."

I smiled, thankful for her unwavering bravery and strength. "I am not sure what the items are, but I know they are buried under each of the beds, so as soon as we reach the teepee, we will need to dig them up."

"This whole thing gives me the jitters." Kenna cringed. "Entering an unknown village, yet knowing we are already familiar with these people, and they with us . . . what if we mess up and say the wrong thing? Will that not make it clear we are aware of their spell?"

I reached out and took my little sister's hand. "We just have to act as we usually would and say whatever comes to mind. I am certain that, however many times we have re-started this loop, it all works out the same in the end, or else it would not be continuing as it has. Honestly, I think what rattles me the most is not knowing how many times we have actually been reset."

Kenna shivered and rubbed her arms. "Oh my, when you put it like that . . . it is definitely not something I want to think about."

Jeremiah moaned, reclaiming our attention. "What happened?" He sat up, holding his head.

"You fell ill, in a way, and I had to cast a spell to find out what was affecting you," I quickly explained.

"And . . ."

"*And*, I discovered that we have all been caught in a time loop cast by the tribe's shaman."

Jeremiah took the damp cloth from my hand and ran it over the back of his neck.

"You are certain?" he asked calmly. Like the rest of us, he was completely used to magic and mayhem continually affecting our lives.

"Yes. The more we discussed it, the clearer things became to us both. Like distant memories—moments of past or already lived events—and feelings about people and families we have yet to meet. But most importantly, there are three cursed objects placed under the beds in the teepee we will be assigned to, which are maintaining this loop." I paused, dreading my next question. "Have either of you felt Karina or had a desire to find her?" They both shook their heads, confirming my suspicions. "I think our quest has somehow been blocked by the shaman's spell, and more likely than not, it is affecting our memories as well."

Jeremiah nodded and tossed the rag atop a stack of pans in the back corner. "Then let's not dally. The sooner we arrive and get to the bottom of this, the sooner we can get back to wherever it is we're truly supposed to be and find Karina."

Without another word, Jeremiah climbed back through the front opening, reclaimed the reins and released the handbrake.

Kenna and I remained in the back, taking in the wild landscape through the hole in the tarp. The sun crept over the distant mountains once again, revealing the same snow-covered peaks I had seen in my vision. The evergreens reaching far into the sky now seemed familiar, glistening with a coat of frost in the late spring morning. I pulled my jacket further up my neck to combat the chill in the air as Jeremiah continued to work the oxen around the final curve in the ascending trail. Yanking hard on the reins, he brought us to a sudden stop, shifting the pots and pans in a cacophony of motion. Neither Kenna nor I made a peep, however, because we both knew what was coming next.

# CHAPTER 7

KARA

"*M*aiku!" The chief spoke directly to me again, offering his usual greeting in his native tongue.

I cast my language spell again and replied, knowing my words were correct and matched the others I had previously spoken in this situation. "Hello. We are the Vargas family and have been approved to trade with your tribe."

"I am Chief Aquakawwa. We have been expecting you. Please follow me." The chief motioned his men ahead, and then led us to the northernmost point in the village, just like before. Jeremiah and I exchanged nervous glances as he climbed from his perch and tied up the oxen, releasing them from the wagon's tongue.

"Get settled, then come to the main dwelling in the center of our village once the sun begins to set. All here are aware of your visit, and I can assure your safety. You are my welcomed guests."

Jeremiah crossed his arms and nodded to the chief, standing still until he and his men rode from sight. Not waiting for him to call us down this time, Kenna and I raced into the teepee and immediately scoured the earth under each of our beds.

"Kenna, grab some of those tools." I pointed to a pile of digger sticks and stone trowels lying against the far wall.

"Here." Kenna handed us each something to further our progress and returned to her designated spot, working furiously until she had a long tract of upturned dirt in front of her, despite the smudges it created on her cotton petticoat and stockings.

"Did you find anything?" Jeremiah asked, settling back on his knees.

"No, not yet. Did you?" I replied.

"No. How about you?" Jeremiah lifted his chin at Kenna.

"Nothing here, either." Kenna threw her digging stick to the ground. "Damn it! The shaman must have moved them this time around."

Jeremiah turned to me. "You said these objects are feeding this loop, correct? So they must be here somewhere," he deduced.

"Yes. That's right." I pushed to my feet, removing my ragged wool coat. "Look around. Search for anything that appears to be out of the ordinary."

Kenna stood with a huff. "Everything here is out of the ordinary. Look at all of this!" Turning in circles, she pointed out the beautifully dyed clothing and handmade items littering the space. "How do we determine what is *out of the ordinary?*"

I walked to meet her in the middle of the dwelling and took both her hands in my own. "With a spell, of course. That should make things a little easier, don't you think?"

Magic sparked in her eyes and tingled between our joined fingers as I cast a quick spell.

*"Goddess of old, lend us your sight, open our eyes, to see as you might.*
*Through altered time, unveil unto me, hidden objects, so mote it be."*

A gust of wind blew through the flap of the teepee, lifting our hair and drawing us all outside. A tiny shimmer of light sparkled before us, leading the way on a swirl of chilled breeze. Following its path, we crept toward the back of the teepee, then bent down as the spark settled in a pile of leaves at the base of the structure.

"Here." I pointed, pushing away the leaves to reveal a mound of freshly dug dirt.

Jeremiah shooed me and Kenna to the side, protective as always. "Let me."

With his roughly crafted spade, he dug into the fresh loam, tossing tiny piles to the side until he uncovered a tightly wrapped object. It was sealed within a skin and bound by twine with bones and feathers weaved into its knot.

"I think we found what we are looking for," he surmised.

I moved forward, grabbing Jeremiah by the arm.

"Do not touch it." Reaching out, I closed my eyes and held both hands slightly above the object, scanning for any ill intent. I concentrated, letting my magic read the energy that was used to forge the talisman. "The magic here definitely has pure roots, but it has been tainted for a darker purpose."

"Well, that's not good," Kenna stated the obvious. "What do we do?"

"I am not certain at the moment. We need to understand what this is. We need more time to determine what kind of spell was cast before we can create a counter-spell of our own to negate its power. With all that being said, I am terrified that when we go to sleep, this whole damn loop will start all over again."

"And back to square one we go." Jeremiah stood and crossed his arms.

"Exactly." I lifted a brow.

"Goodness me. Then let us get it inside so we can get started," Kenna prompted, clearly eager to get to the bottom of this as quickly as possible.

I nodded and leaned forward, whispering a quick protection spell, then grabbed the package gently by its edges.

Sneaking quietly back to the front, we all ducked inside, then sat crossed-legged on the ground with the bundle resting in front of us. I slowly unwrapped the package, carefully sliding the bone and feather from the twine, then gingerly plucked at the edges and pulled back the exterior skin.

Each of us gasped and stared at three glowing stones hidden within. One was a ruby, pulsing bright red; one, a rose quartz, shining a beautiful pink; and the last, an amethyst, radiating a deep violet glow.

"That was not what I was expecting," Jeremiah confessed.

"Nor I." I leaned forward, placing my hands above the stones, and began another chant.

*"Stones of earth, stone of old, rid yourself of your evil goal. Cleansed by the goddess and her servants three, as we will it, so mote it be."*

When nothing happened, I nodded to Kenna and Jeremiah who immediately joined in, intoning the spell two more times.

Energy whipped around the room, stirring on an unseen breeze until it reached its crescendo. Tendrils of magic in the color of each individual stone rose in sparkling strands as they lifted into a vortex. I concentrated on the push and pull of the tainted native magic, and finally, the spell snapped, turning all three strands instantly black. Charred dust floated to the ground, and the room immediately settled.

"Wow. So it is done?" Kenna asked. "The spell is broken?"

"I am not sure. I guess we will have to wait and see if things reset in the morning." I shrugged.

"Should we do a remembering spell, just in case?" Jeremiah suggested.

I nodded in agreement and reached out to join our hands. The tingle of magic that remained from the spell we had just worked burst forth past my lips, shooting light out of the roof as my chant took flight.

*"Remember now, remember us three, today, tomorrow, and forever need be. If time resets, our magic trumps thee, straight from the goddess, so mote it be."*

I smiled. "There. That should do it." I released their hands and took a deep breath, grounding myself and releasing any residual magic back into the earth to safely dissipate.

"Should we dress for their dinner now?" Kenna prompted, twirling her hair.

"Yes, I suppose the best thing we can do is continue the evening as if nothing has changed." I reached forward and picked up the stones. Energy pulsed from within them, calling out to each of us specifically. Following the energy, I handed the ruby to Jeremiah, the amethyst to Kenna, and kept the rose quartz for myself. "Let's keep these with us, though. I do not want to chance the shaman getting his hands on them and recharging them in any way."

Kenna and Jeremiah tucked the stones into their pockets and moved off to dress for the evening, while I whispered one last request to the goddess.

*"Goddess of love, goddess of light, protect all those I love this night. Allow us triumph over any threats to thee, as I will it, so mote it be."*

PHAEDRA

I pulled my wings in tight, landing in the nearest tree as I stared at a bright light that had just burst from the top of a teepee in the canyon below. Magic filled the air, and I shivered. This was true power, born of something greater—something divine, and not the usual earth-based magic the natives practiced here. After all my wandering alone, it was their traditions and magic that drew me to the area originally, but now, something had changed, and I would not be leaving until I knew exactly what.

# CHAPTER 8

KARA

"All set," Jeremiah called out as he emerged from the teepee in a pair of dyed pants, a matching beaded vest, and with a thick fur slung over his shoulders. He gestured to the worn footpath in front of us and took the lead without a single misstep. "Here we go again."

"Are we all good?" I asked, holding up my stone before dropping it into a small skin pouch I had tied to my side.

Jeremiah and Kenna both held up their stones, each clutching them tightly as we started down the path. I drew in a deep breath. "Smells good. Let us enjoy the food but be sure to maintain vigilance. Do you both remember what happens in there?"

"Yes. I've already produced the salve for the gift exchange." Kenna patted the small jar tucked into the folds of her dress.

"Yes. I remember, but what do we do if things go awry? What if the shaman realizes we have broken his spell?" Jeremiah asked.

The drums sounded at that exact moment, bringing *another* ominous end to our short walk.

"I guess we will just have to wait and see." I shrugged.

Jeremiah pulled back the flap of the oversized teepee, and the pounding beat of the drums assaulted us again. Smoke drifted from a fire pit in the center, while members of the tribe were dressed in their elaborate headdresses and seated around the perimeter of the gathering just as before. Chief Aquakawwa stood, and the drums fell silent.

"Welcome, friends. Please sit."

Jeremiah, Kenna, and I walked forward and took our seats upon the blanket-covered log.

"Tonight, we welcome you into our village and celebrate your arrival with the Ute Bear Dance . . ." The drums picked up again, and dancers moved into formation as the chief's words trailed off.

We all sat quietly, straining to appear interested in the show. But just as before, my focus flickered nervously back and forth between the dancers, the chief, and the shaman. I squinted and watched as he continued to work his spell. Frustrated, he blew a third puff of smoke over the herbs in his small bowl, but the ingredients remained benign. No flames rolled, and the magic I had felt before never began to rise. The shaman's head snapped up and caught my eye.

"He knows," I whispered.

Holding his stare, I sat still while Kenna quickly chanted a spell of her own.

*"Words on the wind, float to us three, allow us to hear any plans to harm thee."*

A puff of smoke escaped the fire, as if a dragon had just released a breath that carried Kenna's words toward the heavens. We all quickly turned back to the dancers, keeping the shaman and chief visible in our periphery. However, when the shaman stood to speak to the chief, his voice now drifted clearly to our ears.

"The spell has been broken. We no longer have the witch's magic to protect us here. The time loop is at its end." The shaman turned, then exited out the back of the teepee, leaving us surrounded by warriors when the chief raised his fist to stop the celebration.

## PHAEDRA

Balanced on the lodge poles of the nearest teepee, I watched as the tribe's shaman scurried away from the gathering being held below. Hurriedly, he shuffled down the path and walked straight toward the dwelling the newcomers had just recently left. Ripping back the flap, he entered unimpeded. I glided to the top of the structure with a pump of my snow-white wings, and then peered down through the top flap to continue my investigation.

The shaman was frantic, tossing clothes and furs, upending their beds, and throwing tools and dishes against the far walls. Finally, out of breath, he stood in the middle of the room and began to chant and shake his rattle. The sounds of the beads, feathers, and bones raked through the air like claws ripping at the sky. Tainted magic radiated up and out of the opening, blasting me to the ground as I covered my ears in pain.

KARA

Jeremiah stood in front of us, arms crossed over his chest.

"What is the meaning of this?" he asked, taking in the warriors surrounding us.

Surprisingly, Chief Aquakawwa pushed through the men, waving them off and dismissing the entire crowd. "Return to your homes. There will be no feast tonight."

All the natives shuffled to leave, casting curious glares in our direction—some worried, some sad, and even some angry.

"I am sorry," the chief offered. "It is clear you now know what my shaman has done."

I stepped around Jeremiah, pulling Kenna close to my side. "We know we have been trapped in a time loop but are unsure how or why." My words were short and direct but left no room for misinterpretation. I wanted an explanation, and I would not be leaving without one.

Chief Aquakawwa gestured for us to retake our seats, folding himself to the ground in front of the fire. "I will explain the best I can."

With protection spells at the ready, we all sat and listened intently.

"A few years ago, the Ute and Comanche began negotiations to ensure peace between our two powerful tribes that controlled the southwestern plains. However, peace talks were interrupted, and since then, war has threatened us all." The chief shifted uncomfortably on the ground. "When our shaman sensed your arrival, your well of magic called to him, and the idea of utilizing your power to safeguard our tribe took root in his heart." He met my eyes with an intense gaze. "I did not understand his true purpose at the time, but once I saw his spell working, I had no idea how to break it." He lowered his chin. "Nor did I want to." Shaking his head and freeing his guilt, he looked up at us and continued. "He protected our home and people, and as chief, that is my one and only goal. I had no idea he would have to siphon your magic to do so, and for that, I am sorry."

"What do you mean, siphon our magic?" Kenna snapped, sparks playing at her fingertips.

"While trapped in the time loop, your memories were lost. You have not performed magic in all the seasons you have been here, and without it, your powers have started to drain. Only when your minds fully break free do you regain full access to it and can you start casting again."

"Wait. How many *seasons* has it been, and why do we not remember the rest of our time spent here?" I asked, desperate to obtain as much information as possible.

The chief took a deep breath. "Your lives here progress normally until you begin to recall other memories, at which point, the shaman resets the loop to start again, wiping all your previous experiences from your mind." He swallowed hard. "It has been three seasons."

Kenna jumped up. "What? We have been stuck in this loop for nine months?"

I stood and grabbed Kenna by the arm, trying to calm her while I explained as much as I understood.

"Yes. It is why we are remembering the others of the tribe and working in the fields during the summer." I turned to the chief. "From what you have explained, I assume we only *reset* whenever our memories break free, which brings us back to this initial starting point each time, correct?"

Chief Aquakawwa pushed to stand, addressing us each and spouting his apologies. "Lorenzo, Clara, Catalina. I am sorry, but yes, that is correct. Once it begins again, the rest of us are also pulled in, and as I have explained, I had no knowledge of how to break the spell."

Kenna yanked her arm from my grasp and strode to the opening of the teepee and tore back its opening. "Well, we did break the spell, and now, we're going to make sure this never happens again." She jerked her chin at Jeremiah and me. "Come on. We have a shaman to find."

# CHAPTER 9

KARA

*R*acing from the teepee, Kenna pounded down the path that would lead us back to our assigned dwelling. She stopped dead in her tracks, however, when she caught sight of two wolves stalking around a prone figure lying on the ground directly in front of us.

"Go on, get out of here!" Jeremiah shouted at the wolves, pushing past us and waving his arms in the air.

"No. Wait." I grabbed him and walked forward. "These are not normal wolves, and that *isn't* a person wrapped in white coverings."

Kenna joined me, and I immediately felt it when she sensed the same magic I had. I looked around, making sure we were alone, and quickly cast a spell.

*"Cloak us now, from mortal sight. Hide their vision, though try they might. Allow us to talk safely within, protect this haven as we greet new friends."*

A shimmering bubble burst forth, encapsulating us all within it. Under the protective dome, our true selves became visible instead of the Vargas façades we currently wore.

"Hello. We are the Howe witches from Salem, Massachusetts, and have been brought here through our soul journeys. Is the angel going to be well?" I asked, fully aware of the divine being lying before us.

The three of us remained still as the two wolves began to shake. They shed their pelts within seconds, reclaiming their true form, standing naked before us, completely unabashed.

"Greetings," the male replied with a tilt of his head. "We are Ric and Gaby Kasun. And yes, I think she will be fine."

Gaby, a stunning woman with long black hair, silver-gray eyes, and an exotic oval jaw line, bent down and ran a hand over one of the angel's snow-white wings.

Stirring slowly, the delicate angel rose from the ground. Stark white hair fell over her beautiful, yet sullen face, while crystalline blue eyes roamed over each of us from between the strands. There was a sadness about her that somehow darkened the space in which she stood.

"Hello, my name is Phaedra." She smiled kindly at us all, but her voice rang with a sadness that had me clutching my chest as we all introduced ourselves again. "I was drawn here by your magic." She nodded to Kenna and me. "But after witnessing the shaman's attempt to reclaim his power, I was knocked to the ground."

"You saw the shaman here? He did this to you?" Jeremiah asked.

"Yes. He ransacked your teepee, obviously looking for something, but when he did not find it, he cast another spell, which was tainted and forceful. Its off-balance resonance knocked me from my perch above."

Ric Kasun, standing broad-shouldered and at least six four, looked up at the top of the lodge poles sticking out of our teepee and shook his head. Black hair, silvery-blue eyes, and a slight scruff along his jaw painted the picture of a hardened mountain man, yet his concern for the situation rang with the sincerity of a true protector. "Sounds like we need to find this shaman before he hurts anyone else."

"Our thoughts exactly," Kenna replied, then with a swipe of her hand, clothed the Kasuns.

Phaedra and the Kasuns followed us into our teepee, and we began our preparations.

"I could take flight and look for him in the surrounding forest," Phaedra offered.

"Not to offend, but we have been here for a very long time and know the territory well. It would be quicker for us to shift and track him through the woods," Gaby stated flatly, pulling on the hem of the cotton shirt Kenna had produced without asking.

Clearly dejected, Phaedra lowered her head. "You are probably right. Besides, I never fly low enough for people to see me, so looking for him visually would be a waste of time."

Jeremiah shifted next to me, and knowing him as I did, I could tell from the look on his face he would not want the angel to feel unneeded in the situation, so it was no surprise when he piped up again. "No, but you could take to the sky and see if you sense any further use of his tainted magic."

This earned him a quick nod and a small smile from the petite beauty.

"Of course. I could do that," Phaedra replied.

Jeremiah smiled and returned his attention to the Kasuns. "If you have been here that long, have you ever had dealings with this tribe before?"

"No." Gaby reached for her mate's hand. "Ric's mother and our last alpha, Adele, sacrificed her life to get the pack out of Croatia and the blood feud that threatened our family there. She sent us here, to this specific territory in the New World, where we've remained disguised as a roving native tribe. We've spent our time fostering peace with everyone we have encountered in the surrounding areas."

"While that sounds fantastic, and I am so grateful we have met, can we get down to business?" Kenna interrupted. "We need to locate the shaman as quickly as possible and strip him of his power, so let's have Phaedra take to the skies, and you and Ric track him through the forest. Whoever finds him first, simply crush this in your hand, and we will be brought straight to you." She held out what appeared to be two small pieces of fruit.

"What?" I asked.

"Yes. I have charged them with a locator spell. Once they are crushed, I will draw upon the magic of this land to transport us there."

"No. That is not what I mean. What I mean is, *what are you saying*—that you want to strip him of his power? How can we do that to someone whose magical traditions run so deep?"

"Kara. We need to make sure he does not inflict this time loop on us or anyone else *ever* again," Kenna replied matter-of-factly, extending me her hand.

I shook my head and pushed to stand. "I know we are only visitors here, pulled out of our lives and time, but after all we have learned about the natives in the nine months we have lived among them, you are okay with stripping them of their ancestral magic?" I pushed her hand away. "Because now that I can remember our time here, I'm not sure I am comfortable with that plan."

Kenna stood still, shocked and staring at me as I turned and stomped outside.

"I will go talk to her," I heard Jeremiah offer.

"Let me." Gaby's voice drifted from behind me, then called out, "Kara, wait . . . please?"

I stopped a few feet away but did not turn around. Staring out at the surrounding forest, I remained quiet, knowing I would be forced to listen to whatever the alpha wolf had to say.

"I understand your concern. I, too, would normally fight against your sister's plan. Unfortunately, there is a greater good at play here. Once a shaman's magic becomes tainted such as this, things will only worsen. I have seen it before. His spells will cause the tribe to suffer, and any and all prosperity bestowed upon them will start to fade away as a punishment for his actions." She laid a hand gently on my shoulder. "If you want to truly save these people, you will need to do this."

"I know. The threefold law." I wiped a tear from my cheek and followed Gaby back inside, but continued to contemplate an alternative as I struggled to look my baby sister in the eye.

## SHAMAN

"No one understands," I mumbled, cutting a trail through the forest and slipping on the remaining ice and snow still gathered in the shadows of the massive evergreens. I trudged over rocks and stumps, fleeing the village, and listened for the rumble that would announce the Great Falls up ahead.

Dropping almost three hundred feet from a dip in the cliff above, the falls poured into a large pond, surrounded by boulders where the canyon met the base of the mountain. Its power and beauty left all who ventured here with an overwhelming sense of magic and peace.

Rounding one final corner of the trail, the pond came into view, its churning water easing my despair. Kneeling, I gave thanks to Great Spirit—the creator of things including the mountains, rivers, people, and animals—and poured out my soul. "Great Spirit, I call to thee. Allow my magic to take root again to protect our tribe from the outside world. Keep us safe within our haven and help maintain the spell I placed upon the witches. My intent was not to harm, only to protect. I did this for my chief and our people, and no one was hurt by my actions. They are out of their time; nothing will be affected by their absence. The witches lived happy lives here until their memories resurfaced. I do not know what went wrong. I reset the time loop, and everything had fallen back into place . . . until now. How did they break through my spell? I need your help, Great Spirit. It is said you created all things when you grew bored with life in the sky and drilled a hole through which to see the world below. I ask that you see me now and hear my plea."

Blood spilled as I pulled my knife across the neck of the rabbit I had brought along as my sacrifice. Its thick life force dripped onto the ground, cutting a trail through the rotted leaves and creeping its way toward the water's edge.

I sucked in a breath, shocked when the water in the pool recoiled from its banks. The blood turned to inky wisps and evaporated into thin air as a great sigh resonated from the sky. I closed my eyes as a powerful wind blew into my face—no doubt a message that my request had been heard. With my hope restored, I opened my arms wide and waited to be blessed by the Great Spirit.

# CHAPTER 10

PHAEDRA

*I* took to the sky and flew in circles above the clouds as I focused on the energy radiating from the forest below. Every living thing cast a unique signature, so it did not take long for me to sense where something was wrong. Soaring to the highest point in the area, I pinpointed the shaman and flew down in a great gust with a pull of my wings. Landing on a large boulder next to the base of the Great Falls, I called out, "Shaman! You have tainted the magic of your people, and for that you will now be punished."

Just as the red piece of fruit materialized in my hand, the shaman disappeared.

## SHAMAN

Surrounded by clouds, I smiled widely as a heavenly scene formed before me. Stark white teepees as far as the eye could see lined a beautiful valley—lush with green hills, flowering trees, and bubbling waterfalls and rivers. Smoke rose from a large sweat lodge at the center of the scene, piercing my senses with the smell of sage, cedar, and sweet grass. It was then I realized that I was in the Sky World, the realm of the Great Spirit.

Shuffling forward as quickly as my old legs would allow, I walked to the dwelling and entered with my head bowed in reverence. "Great Senawahv, thank you for hearing and listening to my plea, and for allowing me to visit your heavenly realm. I am greatly honored."

Another heavy sigh drifted to my ears, this one of sorrow and disappointment. I moved to lift my head but found myself held in place, unable to gaze upon the Great Creator. Suddenly, I was forced to my knees, and the Great Spirit's voice boomed, filling the space.

"Tainted magic, devious plots, and the spilling of innocent life will never be rewarded by me. Only your good intentions are saving you this day. However, you *will* face punishment, albeit not by my hand. Return now and plead your case, for your future rests with those from the past."

The surrounding vision faded into the clouds, and I found myself back in the main teepee of our village, standing directly in front of my chief.

## PHAEDRA

I spun around, looking for where the shaman had gone, then took to the sky and continued to glide over the Great Falls. I spotted the Kasuns stalking toward the water from the forest and quickly returned to the ground, landing again on the large boulder.

"I had him. He was there," I pointed, "but then he just . . . disappeared."

With teeth bared, the Kasuns combed the area, sniffing and rifling through underbrush near the river's edge. Shifting into her human form, Gaby quickly announced, "He killed something right here."

"If he has resorted to killing, then stripping him of his magic may not be enough of a punishment," Ric added, after shifting to join her.

I snapped my wings closed and stalked toward the wolves. "I do not like the idea of killing."

"Nor do we, but you saw it with your own eyes—you said he disappeared, which means his powers are growing. He has to be stopped," Ric replied.

"I am not sure that is a decision any of *us* should make. The decision should remain with the witches he has cursed." I pushed into the sky, hovering over the wolves. "Let's return to the village and let them know he has escaped."

# CHAPTER 11

## CHIEF AQUAKAWWA

"*C*hief. I . . . I have been returned to explain . . ." Shock muddled my shaman's words.

I spun to face him—the man I'd trusted with the welfare of my people since the formation of our tribe. "How dare you return to this sacred place! You have put all our people in danger with your selfish works, and now you are being hunted."

"Hunted? By whom?" he asked, clearly unaware of what had transpired here.

"Who do you think?" I snapped. "The witches you have cursed will find you soon enough, and there is nothing I can do to stop them." I walked forward and laid a hand on his shoulder. "You have brought this on yourself, old friend, and unfortunately, we are now all in line to pay for your mistakes."

"No!" he shouted, shrugging off my hand and stomping to the raised platform where he traditionally worked his magic spells. "The Great Spirit told me I could return and plead my case—to explain that my intentions were pure." He pulled his medicine bowl into his lap and dumped in a handful of herbs, his brow wrinkled in concentration.

"Perhaps that would have made a difference before you killed an innocent living thing," a voice sounded from the opening. I turned to see a woman and man stalking forward. Without another word, their bodies shook, and suddenly a pair of wolves replaced their human forms.

"Great Spirit!" I stumbled backward, turning toward my shaman. "He has sent his hounds to collect your soul."

"Stop!" another voice echoed from the doorway.

I sank to my knees and whispered, *"The White Woman . . ."*

"Yes, you see, a gift! The Great Spirit sends me an angel from above," my shaman called out, still clinging to the hope of redemption.

The White Woman stepped forward. "No. I am not from your Great Spirit, nor do I come bearing a gift—only a message, and a sentiment I am sure your Great Spirit shares. Your magic *was* the gift, given to you by Mother Earth, and you have ruined it, placing your tribe at risk through your selfish deeds. You know as well as I that when power is used to harm in *any* way, there is always a price to be paid."

My shaman shook his head, fighting back his fear and desperation as he struggled to complete his spell.

The White Woman lifted her hand, producing a piece of fruit, then crushed it between her fingers. "It is time for you to face those you have cursed."

I crouched low, remaining still, as the wolves crept closer to my shaman. Suddenly, a bright light appeared in the center of the teepee, and all three witches stepped out of what seemed to be a tear in the air.

With a flick of her wrist, Catalina turned my shaman's entire bowl to dust. "You have ripped us from our time, cursing us as you siphoned our magic, and doomed your people in the process. For this, you will pay."

Clara stepped in front of her sister. "Are we really doing this? Are you sure there is no other way?"

"He killed a rabbit in the forest," the White Woman interjected. Lorenzo's gaze snapped to me. "I thought all living things were cherished by your people."

"They are." I lowered my head, silently giving them permission to proceed.

"The Kasuns believe he should suffer the same fate." The White Woman lifted her chin at the wolves as a tear shimmered down her cheek.

Shifting back to their human forms, the wolves remained stoic and unapologetic. "As I told Kara," the female wolf lifted her chin, "I have witnessed this before. Once a shaman's magic becomes tainted, things will only grow worse. Livestock will start to die, crops will no longer produce, even illness may threaten the tribe. It is in everyone's best interest to end the . . . threat."

Silence filled the teepee as the inevitable sank in.

Slowly, Lorenzo and the male wolf moved toward my shaman, and there was nothing I could do to stop them.

"Wait. There has to be another way. Can you do a spell to cure him?" the White Woman pleaded. "Use your magic to heal his?"

Lorenzo reached out to the male wolf, grabbing him by the arm. "Hold on. That just might work."

Catalina released a tendril of her dark hair and turned to her sister, taking her hands in her own. "I'm willing to try, but if it doesn't work, we put an end to this. Agreed?"

"Agreed," Clara replied, a small smile lighting her eyes. "This will take some time, though, so I suggest we all prepare for a long night." She turned to me, those same piercing eyes that first caught my attention softening as she bowed her head. "Chief Aquakawwa, I hate to ask, but may we have that meal now?"

I looked at my shaman being held in place on his knees. Although facing punishment, he was still safe and sound. So, with a sharp nod, I exited the teepee, happy to provide sustenance to those willing to save his life.

KARA

With everyone fully clothed again—thanks to Kenna—and all with full stomachs—thanks to the chief—Jeremiah and Ric cleared the plates of dried meat and fresh vegetables off to the side, as Phaedra and Gaby positioned the shaman's body on the ground near the fire. I had cast a sleeping spell upon him in order to make his aura more pliable to the work we would be doing here tonight. However, we were now on our third attempt, and my hands were beginning to shake.

I spread them over the shaman's body again and tried my next spell.

*"Heal the heart, heal the mind. Combine our magics over time. Reverse the darkness rooted in he, as I will it, so mote it be."*

*Damn it! Nothing.* I threw the small charm bag clenched in my fist to the ground, spilling the herbs from within.

"Let's try the stones," Kenna suggested, retrieving the amethyst from her pocket.

Holding out her hand, she waited for Jeremiah's ruby, then bent down to add both to the rose quartz already resting in my palm.

I stared at the stones, suddenly entranced. "No. I do not think that is a good idea."

A vision filled my mind, pulling me out of time again. People, dressed in what looked to be costumes of some sort, milled around a quaint little town filled with colorful tents in brilliant shades of red and green, while a kaleidoscope of brightly colored signs advertised Tarot readings, palm readings, and psychic interventions.

"Why? What do you see?" Kenna asked.

I closed my eyes and focused on the three women filling my mind's eye, the most prominent a redhead who looked strikingly like our mother. She held a stone within her hand, and her heart ached to help lovers who had also been ripped out of their time. "My family . . . in need. Here . . . in this canyon . . . but different. In a different time." I shook my head, freeing myself from the vision, and stared intently into my sister's eyes. "We cannot use the stones for this."

"Okay. We will think of something else." Kenna spoke softly, knowing not to question my visions.

"Why do you think your magic's not working?" Gaby asked.

"I am not sure." I stood and shook out my tired arms.

"Perhaps he needs to be awake after all," Jeremiah suggested.

"Perhaps, but honestly, I fear it is just too late. I think his magic is leaving him, and there is nothing left for us to heal." I brushed off the front and back of my dingy skirt and began to pace.

"Or maybe it's his spirit that is fighting you," the chief interrupted from the corner. "As an elder and a shaman, he possesses powerful protection magic. His inner bear may be fighting to survive."

"That is a really good point," I conceded. "All right, let's wake him up."

# CHAPTER 12

KARA

*W*ar cries tore through the village, piercing the air as pounding hooves and battle drums sounded outside.

"What is happening?" Kenna shouted.

"The Comanche! We are under attack!" Chief Aquakawwa pulled a hatchet from his belt and ran out of the teepee and straight into the fray.

Ric Kasun poked his head out the opening, but quickly pulled the heavy flap closed, securing the entrance with the cross beams that lay on the ground next to the door. "Looks like the outside world has finally come crashing back in."

"What do you mean?" Phaedra asked, wrapping her snow-white wings around herself and sliding as far away as possible from the chaos outside.

"While the tribe and witches have been stuck in their time loop, the outside world continued to turn. The Comanche have no doubt been searching the area for this village, only to find it once the spell was broken," Ric quickly explained his theory to the entire crowd.

"This cannot be happening right now!" Kenna threw her arms in the air.

"Well, it is. Which means we have an immediate problem to deal with if we all want to survive the night." Gaby nodded to her husband as smoke began to seep across the ground. "They are going to burn this village down. We need to split up."

"Wait. You are not going to help them?" Jeremiah asked. "I thought you spent your time fighting for peace across these lands."

"Fighting for peace, yes. Not for blood."

Flames made their way under the thick skin of the structure. "Go now, while you still have a chance. If we do not find you again, just know it was a pleasure meeting you all." Gaby and Ric shifted into their wolf forms and slid out the back opening, blending smoothly into the night.

"Well, isn't that just great!" Kenna threw her hands in the air.

"Gaby is right. It is not our place to interfere with their history." Phaedra turned to follow the Kasuns, but stopped and stared at me with her sad eyes. "I have been wandering a long time, and know that love is the only thing that truly can make a difference." She nodded toward the pink stone still lying in my hand. "Follow your heart, and you will find a way."

I stared, blankly, as Phaedra pulled her wings in tight and slipped through the back flap, taking flight the moment the night engulfed her.

Thick poles crashed to the ground as fire ate up the sides of the canvas.

"Come on," Jeremiah yelled, heaving the shaman's body over his shoulder. "We have to get out of here. The teepee is coming down."

Left with no other choice, we followed Jeremiah out the back opening and crept into the nearby trees.

Screams of war and shrieks of terror raked through the air,

shredding the calm that usually layered this peaceful canyon. Thundering horses stampeded through the village, tromping over burned homes and broken bodies. Blood-coated hatchets and knives flew into soft flesh, only to be yanked out and cast through the air again and again.

Plastered to the ground and hidden in a ditch, Jeremiah, Kenna, and I caught glimpses of the chief and other warriors of the Ute tribe fighting valiantly, slaying numerous Comanche as they defended their homes. But in the end, it was not enough, and we were forced to watch helplessly as the entire tribe was slaughtered.

KARA

The warmth of the morning sun woke me first. We were still alive and safe within the hidden ditch, thanks to our protective cloaking spell. I shivered and reached out to wake Jeremiah and Kenna. "I do not see anyone. I think it is over."

Jeremiah held up his hand, signaling for me to stay quiet while he rose and evaluated the area. He was no more than ten steps away when Phaedra landed directly in front of him, her white wings spread wide, making for one hell of an entrance. "It is safe. They have all returned to their own territory."

Jeremiah waved us forward then returned his attention to the angel. "I am surprised you came back. Are you all right?"

"Why?"

"You seemed . . . distraught about what we have to do, and again when you were speaking to Kara about love. Is that why you always seem so sad? Did you lose someone close to you?"

With a huff, she shot into the sky without another word.

"What did you say to her?" I nudged his shoulder.

"Obviously, the wrong thing." He shook his head. "Come on, we need to get the shaman and finish this."

"Finish what?" Ric called out from behind us. "Everyone is gone."

He walked forward to meet Gaby, who was already standing over the shaman's body where it still lay within the ditch.

I knelt down next to the shaman, easing him awake. "You are right. And that is another problem we have to fix."

# CHAPTER 13

KARA

"*A*re you sure you want to do this?" Gaby asked.

"Yes. The angel was right. I have to follow my heart, and I *know* if we do it this way, balance will be restored." I smiled at the alpha wolf, then nodded at Jeremiah, signaling we were ready to go.

Taking the shaman by the arm, Jeremiah waited as the rest of us joined him. Kenna, the last to step forward, smiled at me and with a wave of her hand, produced another split in space. Stepping through, we all emerged at the base of the Great Falls, finding Phaedra already waiting atop a giant boulder.

"I am glad you have joined us again." I smiled.

"I am glad you followed your heart," she retorted.

Jeremiah cast another sleeping spell upon the shaman, then carefully laid his body near the pond's edge. Reaching into his pocket, Jeremiah handed me his ruby. "If you are sure."

"I am." I held out my hand to Kenna and accepted her amethyst next.

Finally retrieving the rose quartz from my own pocket, I hiked up my skirt and knelt beside the shaman and began. "Ruby, for contentment and peace." Leaning forward, I placed the red stone on the ground above the shaman's head. "Amethyst to guard against self-deception." Reaching across him, I placed the amethyst in his left hand. "And rose quartz . . . for love." Closing my eyes, I gently pressed the rose quartz into the palm of his right and recast the remembering spell I had used before, this time including the Kasuns and Phaedra.

*"Remember now, remember us six, today, tomorrow, and forever be fixed. If time resets, our magic trumps thee, straight from the goddess, so mote it be."*

A snap of magic sealed my words in place, and it was time to prepare for the next phase of my plan.

"Jeremiah, you kneel above him there," I pointed to the shaman's head, "and Kenna, you next to his left hand, by your stone." Kenna nodded and moved into place across from me. The Kasuns shifted into their wolf forms and lay peacefully on the ground next to the pond, just below the shaman's feet and out of the way, while Phaedra stood still upon the boulder.

With everyone present and all in place, I began the spell that would take us back to the beginning of it all.

*"Forged by magic, old and true, reset the time loop again to renew. Activate the spell within, one last time to save our friends."*

KARA

Jeremiah must have woken before either of us girls and set off on the trail this trader had been traveling over for the last few weeks. Lorenzo, Catalina, and Clara Vargas were our names in this lifetime, and . . .

Kenna interrupted my thought as she jumped up, tossing furs and blankets into the air.

"It worked!" she cried out, startling the two large oxen pulling the wagon across the rough terrain.

"Yes, it seems so," Jeremiah replied from the front, yanking on the reins and pulling us to a stop as Kenna and I both pushed through the opening to join him.

"Do you both remember?" I asked.

"Yes. Everything." Kenna smiled and relayed the visions spilling into her mind—the same visions I'd had before when the spell previously broke. Celebrations, meals being shared, Jeremiah, me, and herself working the fields in a summer that had yet to come. Friends turned family through native customs, all set against the wild landscape in the box canyon they were all so desperate to protect . . . Everything poured back to her, exactly the same as it had been before.

"Me too," I added. "It is time to set things right."

Jeremiah snapped the leathers and released the handbrake, ready to finish our trek to the village.

We rode in silence as the sun crept over the distant mountains. Snow-covered peaks surrounded us again, while the evergreens still strained to reach far into the sky, glistening with a coat of frost in the late spring morning.

"You realize this will be the last time we see this magnificent landscape," Jeremiah stated as he pulled his jacket further up his neck to combat the chill in the air.

"You never know. Maybe one of our soul journeys will return us here at a later date." I shrugged, thinking back to what I had seen within my stone.

"Perhaps, but first, we have to finish this and get back to finding Karina," Kenna added. "I am still upset the memories of her were wiped from our minds by the shaman's spell."

"Me, too. His intentions still do not justify his actions, and maybe it was Karina who reached out and helped us to remember in the first place. Regardless, I know this is the right choice."

"Are we ready, then?" Jeremiah asked.

Kenna and I nodded in unison and climbed back into the wagon, preparing to once again play our parts. Pulling on the handbrake, Jeremiah guided the oxen around the final turn of the ascending trail. With a hand raised to greet our friends—alive again —he slowly pulled the wagon to a stop.

"Maiku!" The chief spoke directly to me as usual as I peeked my head out the front.

Muttering the language spell once more, I replied on cue, "Hello. We are the Vargas family and were sent with approval to trade with your tribe."

"I am Chief Aquakawwa. We have been expecting you. Please follow me." We followed the chief to our familiar structure with tight lips and wide smiles. "Get settled, then come to the main dwelling in the center of our village once the sun begins to set. All here are aware of your visit, and I can assure your safety. You are my welcomed guests," the chief instructed yet again.

Jeremiah nodded and helped us from the wagon, immediately leading us around the back of the teepee to retrieve the stones.

"It is all exactly the same." I grinned, pleased everything was going to plan. I bent down and whispered my protection spell again, then unearthed the package from beneath the pile of leaves, gently grabbing it by its edges and dusting off the dirt.

Walking back inside, we sat crossed-legged on the ground with the bundle resting in front of us, just as before. Slowly unwrapping the package, I carefully slid the bone and feather from the twine and pulled back the skin, revealing our stones within.

Again, the ruby pulsed a bright red, the rose quartz shone a beautiful pink, and the amethyst a deep violet.

*"Stones of earth, stones of old, rid yourself of your evil goal. Cleansed by the goddess and her servants three, as we will it, so mote it be."*

I signaled Kenna and Jeremiah to join in again, and we repeated the spell two more times.

The familiar energy whipped around the room, yanking the tendrils of tainted magic high into the air. With one last push and pull of our power, the shaman's spell snapped, breaking the time loop once more.

"All set." I reached forward, fearlessly gathering the stones, and passed them out to each of us again. "Time for dinner?"

Kenna laughed and reached for a strand of her hair. "Yes, but this time, I am not wearing any of those itchy furs."

# CHAPTER 14

KARA

 enna, Jeremiah, and I reached the oversized teepee before the drums even began to sound.

"Are you ready to do this?" Jeremiah asked.

Kenna and I stood resolute, both poised and prepared to face what we knew was coming next, then nodded for him to continue.

Pulling back the entrance flap, Jeremiah entered first, and we followed, this time dressed in our own travel-worn clothes. Chief Aquakawwa dropped a log in the fire pit, then stood to meet us with his brows drawn tight. "Friends, is something wrong? We have only begun to prepare for tonight's celebration."

"Cancel the celebration. We have come to warn you." I stepped forward, holding out my stone for the chief to see.

Jeremiah crossed his hands over his chest. "We know we have been trapped in a time loop, and understand why, but what *you* do not know, is now that the spell is broken, your entire village is in danger."

A shift from the back of the teepee drew everyone's attention before the chief had a chance to respond.

"What is the meaning of this?" the shaman asked, still clueless to the fact that his spell had been altered again.

"They know," Chief Aquakawwa replied.

"Wait!" I yelled as the shaman moved to run. "The Comanche are coming, poised outside your canyon, and they will wipe out your entire tribe later tonight if you do not let us help you."

"Help us?" the shaman questioned. "Why would you be willing to do such a thing, after what has been done?"

Kenna released a strand of her hair with a flick, stepping forward with a slight curl to her lip. "Because, despite the fact you siphoned our magic to trap us here, we understand that your intentions were true. Do you not trust *our* intentions? Perhaps you need a sign from the Great Spirit that we are telling the truth." Flicking her wrist, Kenna tore open a portal, and out walked Phaedra in all her bright, shining glory.

*"The White Woman,"* Chief Aquakawwa whispered, dropping to his knees.

"Yes. I am here with a message from the Great Spirit. Trust these witches to aid your tribe, and accept your punishment along their side. Foolish were you to attempt such a feat, now fallen from grace, forever you'll be."

I smiled at the angel's delivery of our pre-planned speech, while Kenna kept her eye on the shaman to make sure he was buying our ruse.

Chief Aquakawwa rose and raced to his shaman's side. "Listen to their plea, for I will not let you doom the fate of our tribe."

Accepting his defeat, the shaman lowered himself to his knees. "I will do as the Great Spirit instructs."

"Now, tell us about the Comanche," the chief requested. Standing tall over his shaman, the chief listened as Jeremiah described the impending attack, and how we planned to stop it.

KARA

As the sun began to set, the flap of the teepee opened, and the rest of the tribe filtered in. Chief Aquakawwa raised his hands and quieted the gathering crowd.

"There will be no feast tonight, for there is a much more important task at hand. The Comanche have invaded our land, but with our new friends' warning, we have the time we need to flee the village."

Shocked gasps and angry voices rose at once.

"Why would we flee?" one of the warriors questioned.

"Because this fight not only affects our tribe, but the lives of others. So if we are to remain here, in the heart of this special place, we need to do things differently this time."

Jeremiah, Kenna, and I sat against the far wall behind the shaman, blocking any chance of his escape out the back exit. Phaedra had warned us, before she made her dramatic exit through Kenna's portal, that the shaman still should not be trusted. Sitting quietly while the chief rallied his people to our cause, I rolled the smooth pink stone in my hand.

"We need to hurry," I whispered to Jeremiah.

Jeremiah stood, knowing better than to question me. "Chief. It is time. Gather your people at the Great Falls and stay hidden until the White Woman appears to you again." Laying a hand on the chief's shoulder, Jeremiah leaned in and whispered the last part of his instructions so that only Aquakawwa could hear. "Be sure to not let the shaman out of your sight."

The chief nodded, then led his frustrated and confused tribe from the village and into the surrounding forest. As the last of the warriors fell from sight, Ric and Gaby Kasun emerged from the trees, clothed again with a flick of Kenna's wrist.

"You are sure about this?" Ric asked me, while shaking Jeremiah's hand. Gaby stepped forward and hugged both us girls.

"Yes. This is the way it has to be. Just follow the tribe, and make sure the shaman does not try to escape or cast any more spells. No one can be in the village at the time of the attack," I explained.

"Except for you, you mean." Gaby looked deep into my eyes. "And you are sure the illusion will work?"

I didn't bother replying, but instead, closed my eyes and cast the spell I had previously developed for this exact moment.

*"Time will bend, and time will renew. Protected by us, through and through. Cast the illusion to put history in place, all moving forward with the Spirit's grace."*

Nothing around us changed . . . until we walked outside.

Smoke billowed from the central cooking pit, wafting scents of savory meat and vegetables into the air as families roamed the trails between the teepees. Women and children layered in furs carried plates of food toward the gathering that was supposed to be taking place. Warriors dressed in their celebratory skins practiced the dance they would be performing later tonight. And all of it was a lie.

"Unbelievable." Gaby sighed.

I laughed. "Hopefully, it is *very* believable."

"Oh, it is," Ric replied, grabbing Gaby's hand. "We'll keep an eye on the shaman and make sure no one ventures back from the falls. Be safe."

"Thank you." Jeremiah lifted a hand, then turned to face me. "Do you think we are strong enough without Karina's magic to aid us?"

"I think we will have to be," I replied somberly.

"I wonder where she is in this lifetime? Do you think she is close by? Or have we been pulled so far out of time that our family connection has been severed?" Kenna wiped a tear from her cheek.

"I am not sure without doing our locator spells for her, and unfortunately, we simply do not have time." I patted my sister's hand. "But, as soon as this is all over, it is the first thing we will do. I promise."

War cries and the pounding beat of hooves tore through the village, bringing our discussion to an end.

"It is time." Jeremiah nodded and led us both around the back of the teepee and to the ditch in which we knew we would all be safe.

Watching the attack again was so very difficult. The burning structures were real homes being lost, but thankfully, the tribesmen, women, and children were only figments of reality, created specifically to be destroyed. With history back in line, the tribe would remain hidden in this special box canyon until they moved on by choice, or died out peacefully, for that was the one side effect of my spell. All magic had a price, and the tribe as a whole would still have to pay for the shaman and chief's deception, regardless of their good intentions. The shaman would be stripped of his magic, and the tribe would no longer be allowed to expand and grow.

"It's done," Jeremiah announced as the last Comanche warrior rode away from the village, spelled to never return.

"I will signal Phaedra." I whispered a quick spell, sending my words across the back of a breeze, straight to the angel's ears. "Now, let us conjure up the supplies, so they will be ready to rebuild."

Kenna and Jeremiah smiled, then moved into place as we prepared to cast the spell that would provide the necessary items for the tribe to reclaim their lives here within the canyon. Cupping our hands, we each held our respective stones while connecting to the tribal magic native to this land.

*"God and Goddess, hear our plea, help provide for those in need. Supply what is needed, and nothing more, for the work of the tribesmen shall endure. So mote it be."*

Our stones glowed, each in their vibrant hues as I finished the chant. The materials needed appeared in the center of the village, and a rush of magic blasted back into each of our chests.

Kenna gasped. "Wow! That was amazing. I haven't felt power like that since before we lost Karina."

I shook out my arms, trying to dissipate the buzzing energy running through my veins. "The tribe's magic is definitely powerful and combining it with ours seems to have heightened its reach."

Jeremiah stared at the stone in his hand as the red glow began to fade.

"It will need to be contained," he stated, stone-faced. His gaze snapped to mine. "I know we agreed to strip the shaman of his magic, but what is to stop someone else from tapping into this energy and creating another time loop or wreaking havoc in some other way?"

I looked at Kenna, who simply nodded, agreeing the risk was far too great to take.

# CHAPTER 15

CHIEF AQUAKAWWA

*T*he Great Falls glistened as the night sky filled with stars. Huddled with our families, my tribe and I gathered near its base, awaiting word of our beloved village.

Gasps of awe echoed through the crowd when the beautiful White Woman appeared atop a large boulder in front of us. "I bring word from the witches. The attack is over. You may return to your village, but beware, all has been lost. Provisions, however, will be provided for you to begin again."

I quieted the crowd. "Thank you and thank the Great Spirit for sparing our tribe."

The White Woman nodded, then approached my shaman, holding him back as I led my people into the forest. I made no move back toward them, nor had the need to inquire why, for I knew it was time for the shaman to face his punishment. Before they fell from my sight, however, the witches appeared through the trees, and I wondered if I would ever see my shaman again.

KARA

After completing the spell for the tribe's provisions, Kenna opened another portal that we all stepped through, emerging back at the Great Falls as planned.

"Everything all right?" Phaedra asked, still gripping the shaman's shoulder and playing her role of the *White Woman* perfectly.

Jeremiah nodded, moving closer to the edge of the water just as Gaby and Ric emerged from the forest, still in their human forms.

"Have you decided what you are going to do with him?" Ric asked, lifting a chin toward the kneeling shaman.

"Yes. We know what has to be done." I approached the shaman, who lowered his head, finally accepting his fate. "For abusing the ancient power of this land, he will now and forever be stripped of his tribal magic. Neither he nor anyone in this canyon will be able to wield its power without first proving their worth." I paused and looked between Ric, Gaby, and Phaedra. "But we will need your help to protect it."

Ric looked to Gaby and shrugged. "What can we do?"

"Our time here will come to an end sooner or later, at which point we will continue on our soul journeys and most likely never return here again. We need protectors to stay in this canyon and watch over the magic once we are gone."

Phaedra stepped closer, her sad eyes meeting mine. "I cannot promise to remain in the canyon at all times, but I will return often to maintain a watch over it. I hope that will be acceptable."

I smiled. "Having the *White Woman* drop in now and then would truly be a blessing."

Dipping her head shyly, Phaedra made her goodbyes, and in a display of power and grace, took to the sky and faded from view behind the clouds.

Turning again to the Kasuns, I asked, "Can we count on you, too? You have protected this area for so long, it would be our hope that you would continue to do so, holding this secret in place."

Gaby stepped forward, her chin held high. "Of course. We will stay within the area and continue to protect the magic and people of this land." Shifting into their wolf forms, she and Ric moved to the water's edge, lying down, ready to witness as silent protectors.

Satisfied all would be well after we had gone, I gestured to Kenna and Jeremiah to take their places. "Then it is time."

The three of us surrounded the shaman, holding the stones in the palms of our hands. Closing our eyes, we pulled deeply on our pool of true magic from the goddess and allowed our powers to build. Each stone began to glow, radiating with the natives' magic as our energies combined.

*"Siphon the magic from this man, protect the history and this land. Guarded by the dedicated three, concealed and linked, forever shall it be."*

Repeating the chant three times, we stood still as ribbons of energy flowed from the shaman's aura and into each of our stones.

All three stones pulsed in our hands as we trapped the shaman's magic inside. Flinching, I looked down at my stone as it became hot against my palm. The perfect oval stone—a pale pink in its natural state—suddenly changed, its interior shifting to a milky white, like a cloud forming in its center.

"Why is yours now different?" Jeremiah asked as our spell came to an end.

I closed my eyes and held the stone against my heart,

concentrating on the pull I'd felt from the first time I had touched it.

*"Make your way to my daughter's hand, lending her guidance as fore-planned, give her this message, for she will know what to do, 'Time is fluid, fickle yet true.'"*

I continued to whisper into the stone, leaving a message for a daughter I had yet to conceive.

Kenna gasped, openly shocked. "Well, that is an interesting development!"

Jeremiah moved to support the shaman who was still alive, yet clearly drained.

"A discussion for another time," he stated, helping the elder to his feet. "Let us finish this, so we can return him to the village and prepare to say our goodbyes."

Jeremiah nodded to Ric and Gaby, who stalked forward, standing behind the shaman as we moved into place to complete the last part of our spell.

Nearing the pond's edge, Jeremiah, Kenna, and I looked up at the Great Falls and gathered our magic once more. Holding our arms over the surface, the stones that now contained the shaman's power floated out of our hands and hovered in midair above the water.

*"Magic stored safely within, encased for all time from beginning to end. Mixed with our power, by the witches three. Protect this new aether, so mote it be."*

Kenna and I fell backwards as a massive shockwave blasted from the pond, sending a tube of water straight into the air. Jeremiah stumbled to keep his balance and raced to help us as we watched the water whip around the stones. Within the liquid vortex, bright bursts of pink, red, and purple shot into the swirling mass. Seconds later, the water wall dissipated in a rush, sucking the absorbed magic to the bottom of the pond with it, along with the stones. A stillness hung in the air as a silver tint blossomed just under the water's surface.

"The magic of this tribe, combined with that of our goddess, will now remain in the Great Falls for all time," I explained as I turned to face Ric and Gaby. "Protect it, for it will undoubtedly draw many others to the area."

Ric and Gaby lifted their snouts into the air, confirming their earlier promise, then ran into the surrounding evergreens.

"Let's go," Jeremiah prompted, taking the shaman gently by the arm.

Kenna shook her head, claiming a piece of hair between her fingers. "We will need to walk back to the village. My powers are too drained to tear another rip for us to use."

I placed an arm around my sister's shoulders and fell in line behind Jeremiah as he led the shaman through the thick forest.

"You know, the Utes harvest the inner bark of these pines for their healing compresses and teas." I pointed to the large ponderosas surrounding us, pinpointing the visible scars on the trunks. "Perhaps we could incorporate some of it into Karina's healing tea." I winked. "I think we could all use a magical boost after that."

Kenna smiled and pulled a knife from her thick wool coat, carefully taking just enough to aid in our healing. "Once our energy is restored, we need to discuss what just happened, and also how we are going to get back to our search for Karina."

"Do you not think we could live out our lives as the Vargas family while we search for her here?" Jeremiah asked from a few steps in front of us.

I dropped my head, not ready to discuss the facts of what I knew in my heart to be true. "I am sorry, but we need to return to our true soul journey as soon as possible because . . . Karina is not here." I reached for Kenna's hands again. "Not only did the shaman trap us in his time loop, but we have been diverted away from our original destination in time. If we stay here, we will lose an entire lifetime of searching for our sister."

Kenna stopped on the trail, pulling her hands from mine, and wrapped her arms around her middle. "What does that mean? How are we supposed to trigger our next soul journey, then?"

I took a deep breath and replied, "We will have to die."

# CHAPTER 16

KARA

"Thank you for not killing him." Chief Aquakawwa bowed to us all, and then led the elder to the back of the temporary structure that had already been erected in the center of the village. "You are still my welcome guests here. Please stay as long as you like. A teepee will be ready for you within the hour."

"Thank you." Jeremiah tilted his head to the chief, then walked back to meet Kenna and me, where we stood waiting off to the side. "A place will be ready for us soon. Until then, I think we should find some utensils to brew that healing tea and discuss our plans."

A large fire pit had already been dug outside the gathering tent, where I quickly found three metal cups. "I am surprised they have such modern utensils."

"I'm sure they were traded for during the recent peace treaties." Jeremiah smiled as he poured the provided water into each cup, then waited for me to do my part.

Looking around to make sure we were not being watched, I

opened the clasp on my poison ring—the one I wore at all times. From journey to journey, it never wavered from my finger and held Karina's special blend of healing herbs that she had created long ago. Tipping the dried flakes from within, I filled each cup then snapped the metal closed.

"I miss her so much." Memories of our original lifetime together filled my mind as I stirred the tea.

"I know," Kenna replied. "So do I. But I promise, we will find her soon."

I sniffed the warm brew, its potent notes of angelica root, adder's-tongue, and burdock tickling my nose. "I hope so, but I wish it didn't have to be this way. I am not sure ending the Vargas's lives prematurely is something I can come to terms with."

"What other choice do we have? And how do we know they were not destined to freeze up here during their dealings with the tribe, or be killed in the Comanche raid anyway?" Jeremiah asked as delicately as possible. "I know it sounds cruel, but we cannot tell their future. However, we do know Karina will have one once we get out of here."

I jerked my chin in understanding, then sat quietly and sipped my tea.

As promised, within the next hour a teepee had been set up in the same location as our previous one. Kenna and I rushed inside, anxious to tuck in beneath the warmth of the furs and skins.

"Get some rest, and we will make a plan tomorrow." Jeremiah slid down to a pallet laid out on the ground and crawled beneath its coverings.

I tried to hide the soft sighs and tiny whimpers coming from my cries and heard Kenna doing the same. No further words were spoken as I fell asleep with both hope and dread in my heart as the reality of our plans continued to sink in.

KARA

Soft rays pierced through the tiny holes in the skin of the teepee, creating a dazzling grid of sunlight throughout. I could hear the tribesmen and women already hard at work outside, tightening up the seams and hauling supplies from here to there.

"Good morning," Jeremiah offered tentatively, probably unsure if I would be able to forgive him for what we had to do.

"Good morning." I rose slowly, stretching my arms and back, then walked toward Jeremiah, wrapping my arms around his middle. "Thank you for always looking out for us and putting Karina first."

He hugged me tightly. "Always."

"Okay, okay. Let me in here." Kenna joined in on the quick family hug, then pulled away, rubbing her stomach.

"So, food first, then plans?" she asked, flipping her long dark hair over her shoulder.

"Yes, please." I grabbed a large clay bowl from beside the door. "But first, let me go fetch some water for us to clean up with."

I pulled on my fur hat and exited the teepee, stepping immediately into the flurry of activity racing by outside. Horses pulling large lodge poles pounded near me, while women and children scurried about, gathering any remaining vegetables and berries they could find to restock their food supply. The efficiency with which the tribe had begun to rebuild brought a smile to my face as I made my way to the nearby stream. Bending down, I lowered the bowl into the frigid water and shivered.

"I am surprised to still see you here."

I looked up to find Phaedra standing on the opposite bank. "I could say the same for you." I smiled.

"Yes, well, I wanted to make sure that you truly did follow your heart."

"If you mean did I realize the stone was meant for my future daughter, then yes, I did." I stood. "It called to me from the first time I touched it, and being a rose quartz, it is no surprise the message was buried deep within my heart. I am not sure how or when it will happen, but I now know not to close myself off to future love. Thank you for that."

Phaedra dipped her eternally sullen head. "You are most welcome. I hope you find what so many of us do not." With tears in her eyes, she shot into the sky, fading again into the white fluffy clouds.

Returning to the teepee, I poured some of the crystal-clear mountain water into the cooking pans, then used the rest to clean up and prepare for the hard conversation ahead.

After a quick breakfast, all three of us placed blankets on the ground and sat cross-legged around the small fire Jeremiah had built in the center of the structure. An uncomfortable silence thickened the air.

"I guess I will start," I began. "Before you ask, I have no idea how or why the crystal triggered the message for my daughter. I do not know who she is, or when she will be born, and have received no other information other than the words that came to me from the goddess."

"Do you know how she will get the stone, since it's currently resting at the bottom of the Great Falls pond?" Kenna asked.

"No, I do not. But I am sure other witches will occupy this village in the future and have no doubt that somehow, the stones will find their way to the surface again."

Kenna nodded and winked at me. "Wow! A daughter."

I lowered my head, smiling widely at the unexpected revelation as well.

"With that in mind, our future awaits, though I am not really sure how to approach this," Jeremiah confessed. "This situation is new, and unlike our previous two journeys, we have to contemplate cutting our lives short on purpose." He turned to face me directly. "Do you think this could affect how we travel to our next lifetime, or if by committing suicide, we risk ending our soul journeys here and now, leaving Karina to wander the centuries alone?" He asked the hard question I was sure none of us wanted to face.

I shifted nervously with my head still down and heard Kenna suck in and exhale a deep, exaggerated breath.

"Well, I suppose the first thing we discuss is whether we treat this as a human problem or a magical one," Kenna suggested.

I looked up, my interest piqued. "What do you mean?"

"I mean," she proceeded softly, "we could either take our lives in a multitude of ways like humans do, or we cast another spell that will do the job for us."

Cringing at the thought of taking my own life in *any* way, I pushed to stand. Pacing helped relieve the nervous energy building inside.

"Personally, I do not know of many ways in which to—" I paused, not wanting to use the word associated with such an act. "—accomplish this task, but I would think we could probably make it as simple and painless as possible if we combined the two."

I looked to Kenna and Jeremiah, who both shrugged, obviously unclear as to what I meant.

"For the human element, we could find some hemlock and grind it into our tea, and for the magical side, we can cast a spell that will speed up the process and carry us to our next journey as intended."

"That sounds relatively easy, but again, do you know if by doing this, are we risking the end of our journeys altogether? Besides, does hemlock even grow this high up in the mountains?" Kenna shifted uncomfortably on the ground, scooting closer to the fire in her ragged cotton dress, pulling tight the thick fur covering wrapped around her shoulders. This entire topic brought a chill to the air.

I bent down to warm my hands, answering the second part of her question first. "Yes. While we were at the falls, I noticed some growing in the low-lying area around the far side of the pond."

Jeremiah stood, shaking out, then folding his blanket. "I will retrieve the hemlock, while you two work on the spell."

I held up my hand to stop Jeremiah. "Wait a moment." Then, reaching out to Kenna, I wrapped my arms around her and pulled her close. "Before we begin, how about we contact the goddess and ask her permission to move forward with our plan? If she gives it, we will depart tonight. But if not, we will be stuck here for the natural course of our lives, leaving Karina to fend for herself, wherever she is, until it is time for us to travel again."

Kenna leaned into my shoulder, her small frame shaking as she struggled to hold back tears. "All right."

I held my little sister for a moment longer while she cried, releasing her frustration and fears into the universe, then dabbed her cheeks and positioned myself across from her as we prepared to call out to the goddess.

Holding my sister's hands, I closed my eyes and reached out with my thoughts. "Goddess above, hear our plea. We come to you for permission and guidance, and only with your love and approval will we move forward with our plan."

I didn't have to explain what was in our hearts or minds, for the goddess always knew.

Moments passed, until suddenly a wave of contentment fell over Kenna and me both, activating our heart chakras and radiating a soft glow within our auras.

Kenna's eyes snapped open and a smile stretched across her face. "She approves and understands."

"I had no doubt she would. Karina is the heart of this family, and without her, perhaps it is we who are truly lost." I rose to stand, relieved we would be continuing our soul journeys despite this strange and unfortunate setback, and then walked to retrieve a piece of parchment, a quill, and some ink from our supplies.

"Here." I handed a rough sketch to Jeremiah. "This is what you are looking for."

Jeremiah looked at the drawing, finding a tall, thin stem with small clusters of delicate flowers fanning out at the top. "Okay. I've got it. I will be back as soon as I can."

I turned to Kenna. "So, are you ready to create the spell that will return us to our true time?" I smiled, trying to stay positive despite my own fear.

Kenna reached for my hands, giving them a firm squeeze. "As a matter of fact, I am. I miss Karina too, and if this is what it takes to return us to our soul journey and put us back on the path to finding her, I am more than ready."

I stepped forward and drew her into a hug. "Thank you for always being so strong."

"It is my job," Kenna teased, her confidence restored. "Now, let's get to work."

# CHAPTER 17

KARA

*F*orty minutes later, Jeremiah returned with the hemlock in hand.

"Did you encounter any problems?" Kenna asked, always the protector.

"No. Did you?" He lifted a chin at all the gathered ingredients laid out before us.

"No. We are ready." I stepped forward, taking the hemlock from Jeremiah and mashing it into the three cups I had prepared.

"Should we look for the chief in order to say our goodbyes?" he asked.

"No need. I have asked that he join us here shortly," I replied.

Silence fell as we waited for the chief, each preparing ourselves privately.

"Friends," the chief called out as he entered our teepee, "you called for me? Is your dwelling not sufficient?"

Jeremiah offered his hand. "Everything is fine and much

appreciated, Chief. Thank you for your hospitality and for trusting us to save not only your tribe, but ourselves."

Chief Aquakawwa looked at me, then bowed his head. "You are leaving," he stated somberly.

"Yes. We will be returned to our time, and the Vargases will no longer exist in this one. They will need to be buried once the spell is cast," I explained.

Looking up, Chief Aquakawwa stood tall and lifted his hand, offering us a traditional farewell gesture. "I will return once the sun sets to confirm you are gone, then lay the family to rest. You have my word."

The chief turned and left, leaving us to proceed in peace.

Stepping forward, I passed out the cups, then motioned to the three blankets lying on the ground. "Lie down once you drink the tea. After that, Kenna and I will complete the chant, and . . . that is it."

Taking deep breaths, we each moved into position, sitting first as we raised our cups.

"Wait," Kenna interrupted, "I just . . . I want you to know I love you both so much."

Jeremiah smiled with tears in his eyes, obviously unable to speak past the lump in his throat.

"We love you, too." I smiled. "Now, let's go find our sister."

With confident nods, we all downed the tea, then lay back, ready to complete our spell. Reaching out to Kenna, I clasped her hand.

*"Return us to our journey's end, find our sister, lost again. Use the bond that unites the three, as we will it, so mote it be."*

Three more times we repeated the spell, falling silent as the death tea took its toll. We burst free of our mortal bodies, our energy signatures flying into the cosmos, confirming our spell had worked. Soon, we would be immersed in our new lives and able to continue our search for Karina.

CHIEF AQUAKAWWA

As the sun set, I reentered the teepee to gather the Vargas family and bury them as promised. The hair on my arms stood on end, a result, I was sure, from the remaining traces of magic lingering in the air.

Lifting my arms, I looked to the sky. "Be free, my friends, and know that our remaining time here will be spent well. Thank you for your sacrifice, and for protecting our way of life within this special place. We are the people of the land and will make sure to leave it as pristine as we found it when our time here comes to an end."

Howls sounded nearby as a single white feather drifted down from the opening above, landing directly at my feet. Weaving my way between their bodies, I sang our traditional farewell song and performed a final dance in honor of the witches who had given their lives for my tribe and our uniquely magical home.

# EPILOGUE

## PHAEDRA – 1786

I spotted Ric and Gaby poised on the cliff overlooking the village below. Landing softly next to them, I gazed down into the canyon we had all sworn to protect more than eighty years ago. "It's hard to see the last of them go."

Gaby and Ric remained silent as we watched the current Ute chief prepare the most recent dead. He had cut their hair and washed their bodies, wrapping them with skins and rope to prevent their ghosts from rising. Their homes were then burned, along with their personal belongings, then he buried them atop the ashes in rock-covered graves. Over the last fifty years, the canyon had transformed from a full and thriving village into an eerie, isolated burial ground, high within the mountains. I shivered, never truly getting used to the sight. Beautifully painted teepees had been reduced to ash, replaced by mound after mound of heavy rocks, marking the dead.

The chief—no longer with a tribe to rule—lay down beside the final grave, pulling stones atop his own body as he readied himself to join the Great Spirit as well. We had discussed his options and he promised me—the *White Woman*—that this was his preferred way to go. I watched as he swallowed the hemlock crushed within his fist and sent up a silent prayer when his chest ceased to rise and fall.

"Time will cleanse this special place, wiping away all that has been. The witches foretold there would be others to settle in the canyon here, and I for one plan to honor their wishes and keep it protected and as pure as it should be." I turned to face the Kasuns. "Will you remain, as promised?"

Gaby stepped forward, extending her hand. "Of course. We always keep our word. And while we do not plan to live within the canyon itself, we will remain in the area and protect its secret until our dying days."

I extended my wings, preparing to take flight, when Ric reached out to me. "Will we see you around as well?"

My eyes returned to the canyon below as I thought about the secret that I, alone, now held. A baby—the chief's newborn daughter, born before the witches' spell was cast, that I had smuggled to the nearest Ute village. I, too, had followed my heart, and she was currently alive and well, living safely within a tribe of her ancestors.

I pushed from the ground and hovered slightly above them. "Yes. I am certain you will."

## OPEN TERRITORY – 1854

*We found it. Our slice of heaven on earth. The pull of magic strengthened as soon as we crested the last mountain ridge, and now, we've finally arrived. This secluded box canyon will serve as our haven from the outside world. Surrounded by a thick wood of evergreens, it rings with the sound of a great waterfall in the distance. Now, it is time for us to get to work. Protections need to be cast and then building can begin.*

*We are home.* ~ Anne-Marie Beaumont

~

We hope you enjoyed this story in the Legends of Havenwood Falls series featuring a variety of supernatural creatures. The series is a collaborative effort by multiple authors.
Books in the historical Legends of Havenwood Falls series:

*Lost in Time* by Tish Thawer
*Dawn of the Witch Hunters* by Morgan Wylie
*Redemption's End* by Eric R. Asher
*Trapped Within a Wish* by Brynn Myers (July 2018)
*Blood and Damnation* by Belinda Boring (August 2018)

More books releasing on a monthly basis

Also try the signature New Adult/Adult series, Havenwood Falls, and the YA series, Havenwood Falls High

Stay up to date at www.HavenwoodFalls.com

Subscribe to our reader group and receive free stories and more!

# ABOUT THE AUTHOR

Bestselling and award-winning author Tish Thawer writes paranormal romances for all ages. From her first paranormal cartoon, Isis, to the Twilight phenomenon, myth, magic, and superpowers have always held a special place in her heart. Tish is known for her detailed world-building and magic-laced stories. She has received nominations for multiple RONE Awards (Reward of Novel Excellence), and Author of the Year (Fantasy, Dystopian, Mystery), as well as nominations and wins for Best Cover, and a Reader's Choice Award.

Tish has worked as a computer consultant, photographer, and graphic designer, is a columnist for Gliterary Girl media, and has bylines in RT Magazine and Literary Lunes Magazine. She resides in Arizona with her husband and three wonderful children.

You can find out more about Tish and all her titles by visiting www.TishThawer.com and subscribing to her newsletter at www.tishthawer.com/subscribe.

# ACKNOWLEDGMENTS

Thank you to Kristie Cook for the invitation to join this wonderful world and family. I'm so honored to be here.

To my family: Whether together or separated by miles, Colorado will always be home. The memories we share of our lives there together will always be something I cherish. I love you all!

To Michele G. Miller and Kallie Ross Mathews: Thank you for allowing me to borrow your characters (Ric, Gaby, and Phaedra). They truly helped bring my story to life.

To all my Witches of BlackBrook fans: Thank you for following my Howe witches to Havenwood Falls, so we could finally discover why they were missing from Karina's timeline in Maine, 1703. ;)

A Legends of Havenwood Falls Novella

HAVENWOOD
FALLS
LEGENDS

DAWN OF THE
WITCH HUNTERS

*USA TODAY* BESTSELLING AUTHOR

MORGAN WYLIE

AN EXCERPT

### *Dawn of the Witch Hunters* (A Legends of Havenwood Falls Novella) by Morgan Wylie

Witch hunter Marie Blackstone has always planned to follow in her mother's ways, learning to control her power and live at peace with their coven neighbors. During her first foray into playing ambassador to the witches, she meets Judson Carter. He is everything she wants in a man—and everything her brother hates.

Dante Blackstone has craved power from a young age. After the death of his and Marie's mother, his hatred for the witches grows into madness. For Dante, a witch's mere presence triggers an undeniable urge to end the creature's existence.

Seeking freedom from her brother's vendetta and to find a new way to live, Marie joins Judson and other supernatural beings as they set out in search of a new home and a new way of life. The traveling band makes its way across rough, uncharted terrain, with no idea where they're heading or how long it will take to find the perfect place.

Trouble is inevitable along the way, but for Marie, the worst comes in the form of Dante and his following of rogue witch hunters. They're intent on finding his "lost" family to bring her back into the hunter's way of life—even if that means eradicating any witch who gets in their way.

# DAWN OF THE WITCH HUNTERS

## AN EXCERPT

## CENTRAL VIRGINIA ~ 1840

Barefoot, she walked the path padded with moss from her quaint cottage home to the outskirts of a neighboring village. Cessily Blackstone had a meeting with the leader of an unsuspecting coven of witches. She needed this meeting to offer her the answers she sought. Her time was running short, and she knew it. She could feel it in her bones. Since Sarah Stronghold—the leader about to meet her—had gifted her with the ability to sense not only witches near her but also black magic in her vicinity, Cessily could discern even more within herself. Something dark bubbled in her veins. The town doctor wasn't able to help her. She hadn't told her family yet —her five young children and her beloved husband, Hank—she couldn't imagine leaving them behind. Only time and a visit with the witches—her last resort—would tell.

The grass under her toes sent soothing shivers of joy up her legs, igniting a spring in her step. Though her outlook was grim, she couldn't help but feel the life and strength of the forest around her, longing for her to commune with it. Her long blond hair flowed behind her as she headed toward the meeting place. As she drew closer, the familiar tingling in her arms gained strength. Over time, she had learned to be at peace with the unusual sensations she knew were not human characteristics. Cessily had learned to control the deep desires to seek out and kill a witch—apparently an undesired side effect of the "gift" she had been given to protect her family.

She watched her children closely as they matured. Each had developed varying degrees of the same gift, passed down through her, but thankfully diluted by the joining of her human husband. Except for her second eldest, Rodney, who seemed to be fully human. Part of the gift she'd been given allowed her to sense others similar to her as well. Cessily did her best to keep the children away from the witches until they were ready, but the three eldest—LeAnna, Rodney, and Isaiah—knew of their heritage while the two youngest, Dante and Marie, were still in the dark.

"Cessily, welcome. It has been quite some time since we last spoke," a female voice came from the other side of a tree as Cessily passed by. With a smile on her face, a woman, possibly in her sixties, wearing a long brown but lightweight cloak with a hood over her head, stepped into the pathway. Tall and willowy, she held her chin high and her head proud.

Cessily stopped and inclined her head respectfully. "It has indeed. Thank you for meeting with me, Sarah."

"How can I be of service to you?"

"Is there a way to reverse the gift you bestowed on me?" Cessily sighed. "I mean no disrespect, but I am not sure it is having the intended effect as it is passed down to my children. They are reacting differently, each one."

Sarah frowned, but kept her eyes trained on Cessily, clearly debating something. "No, I'm afraid it is permanent, Cessily."

"Is there anything that can be done to help ease the strongest of the desires for my children? Please don't misunderstand. I am grateful for how you helped me long ago. But I fear for my children. If they are not able to control the gift as I have learned to do, they might let it get the best of them."

"I told you when I awakened this power within you that it would not be an easy road. It is more a responsibility than a gift. You must instruct your children the way I instructed you." Sarah's gaze searched Cessily's face. "What is it you're not telling me, Cessily?"

Cessily scratched at the back of her neck and turned her head slightly, as if listening to something.

"I don't have much time. I think I am dying, Sarah," she said, her voice lowered. "And I've seen darkness in a couple of my children as the gift awakens within them. I'm scared for them."

"Give me your hand," Sarah demanded, holding out her own palm face up. Cessily placed her hand palm up within Sarah's. Sarah studied it, drew her index finger along Cessily's life line, and frowned. A lone tear escaped one of her eyes. "It is true. I am sorry, Cessily."

"Is there anything you can do? Any magic that could delay my end? Anything?" Cessily pleaded, desperation escaping her tone. "I'm not ready to die," she whispered.

Sarah reached out her other hand and placed it tenderly against Cessily's cheek. "I am truly sorry. There is nothing I can do. It is the way of nature, and I cannot interfere, even if I could do something."

"I understand."

"There is more you need to understand . . . more I have not told you about your past, Cessily." Sarah's words were slow, hesitant, with a weight Cessily didn't comprehend.

"What is it?" Cessily frowned and tilted her head, watching Sarah struggle with something internally.

"This gift . . . this power you believe I gave you . . ."

"Yes?" Cessily was concerned. A strange sensation crept up her spine, and chills erupted across her skin.

"I was not the giver. I led you to believe I gave it to you."

"If you did not, who did? What aren't you telling me now, Sarah?"

"No one did. Unless you count your ancestors, that is." Sarah sighed and stepped back from Cessily to gain some needed space. "Cessily, the power you feel, struggle with, gain insight from—your ancestors are the source of it. You are a hunter . . . a witch hunter, to be precise."

"What? You did something, though. I could feel the power flow through me when you blessed me all those years ago," Cessily said, doubt flooding her words.

"Your power was dormant. All I did was awaken the power within you."

"No. I don't believe you. I felt something come alive from your power. Why would I never know about such a huge anomaly in my family? Why would no one ever tell me? My parents never said anything!" Cessily paced, her hands worrying themselves into a frenzy.

"Your grandparents asked my mother, the coven leader at the time, to inactivate their powers when they first arrived here from Europe and to never speak of it again. It took very strong magic. It is all written in this journal I brought for you. My mother had it hidden, but I recently found it amongst her things." From beneath her cloak, Sarah brought out a worn leather book, tied and bound with a long strip of red suede. She held it out for Cessily to take.

Cessily froze, all but her eyes as they took in the little book.

"Could it really belong to my family? Could it hold all the secrets you speak of?" she whispered, but doubt laced her tone. Moving slowly closer, she squinted and peered at the ancient tome. Cessily gasped. Her eyes widened in surprise. "I recognize this symbol on the spine."

Sarah turned it to see the spine, then handed it to Cessily, who examined it more thoroughly. "This cluster of stars on the spine is also on my shoulder and on each of the children except Rodney."

"Then it truly belongs to you," Sarah acknowledged.

"You knew all along then? Back when you offered me a gift of protection?" Cessily frowned, attempting to absorb all the information just thrown at her.

Sarah slowly nodded. "I did. What my nephew . . . what that man did to you, using black magic, was unforgivable. The anger you could have allowed into your soul would have awoken your hunter in an unpleasant way. You would have been overrun with the hunger and desire to hunt and kill all witches. I chose to awaken you in a way to be distinguished as a gift, instead of a reaction to hatred. It allowed you to control and learn your hunting powers more easily. That was my restitution to you, not the actual power."

Cessily gave a small smile. "I still am grateful for the sacrifice and offering you made to me and my family. I might not be here otherwise." She sighed and noted the bright morning sun streaking down through the tree branches, a glimmer of hope in a confusing time. "Do you know much else about my ancestors?"

"It is all in the book. Read it. I will be here if you still want to talk when you are finished."

Cessily nodded. She slanted her head slightly down and to the right, listening, pausing. Her eyebrows pinched, and she bit her lip in concern. "Thank you. I should go. I sense little ones of mine who should not be here."

"Blessed be, Cessily Blackstone."

"Blessed be, Sarah Stronghold." Cessily tucked the book protectively to her chest and headed back toward home.

As she passed the patch of full green shrubbery, she didn't stop and she didn't acknowledge the children except to say, "Best hurry along so your daddy doesn't catch you away from your chores for too long."

Cessily kept walking, enjoying everything around her. The flowers woke to greet the day, the sun warmed the path beneath her toes, and the birds and chipmunks greeted each other with friendly chatter. The bush behind her jostled, and the sounds of running feet thudded away from her. She knew her youngest children, Dante and Marie, would have plenty of questions for her when they next saw her. In fact, Cessily had questions of her own. Skirting by the small trickling creek near their home, she found a nice flat boulder in the sun to sit. So she did, and she opened her family's recorded history—the only one she was aware of—and read.

Within the week, Cessily weakened in both body and mind. Her illness consumed her from the inside out. She had little time left. Her husband Henry Jackson Blackstone—known to his friends as Hank—was one of the most understanding and patient humans she had ever known. He came along her side and lovingly wrapped an arm around her waist, assisting her with his strength. His bright green eyes gazed down upon her face with love and sadness. Her face showed she was slipping away.

"Cess, you need to tell everything to the little ones—share the new information you have learned with them all. Soon," her husband encouraged. He walked with her through the fields behind their cottage with rows and rows of vegetables. Barefoot once more, and as she usually was, Cessily nodded her head in quiet response.

Her family had been excellent farmers before she had grown and married, but Hank had added his expertise of growing grapes to turn into wine. When Cessily married Hank, he understood all she was, including her "extra" abilities. When Sarah, the coven leader, had blessed her with her gifts—or awakened her hunting side, as she now understood—she had made Cessily promise to always keep the Blackstone name prominent in her family. Until now, Cessily hadn't understood those instructions were straight out of her ancestors' book; though she still wasn't sure why, she had kept up the tradition. Hank was so head over heels in love with his new bride, he didn't care what his name was.

"I will tell them tonight. I fear I will not be here much longer, Hank. I'm afraid to leave you and the children behind." Resting her head in the crook of his shoulder, she allowed the tears she had held at bay most of the week to flow.

Everything was happening too fast. She had just found out all about her heritage, and it gave such new meaning to who she was. Was it better to allow her children to believe their abilities were the result of a gift or something that has always been and always would be a part of their lives? It now made sense why her "gift" also functioned at times as a curse, an obstacle she needed to overcome or learn to control. The power, the abilities, the drive—they were all simply a part of her, her nature. If she was honest with herself, she wasn't sure if she would take that nature away from her children, even if she could. Would life be that much easier and better for them if they didn't have to handle being witch hunters? Probably, but it was their family's responsibility, their destiny. Would she change it? No. Would she make it easier if she could? Yes. It was the most challenging part of her nature. But she needed to prepare her children for what was to come.

Made in the USA
Coppell, TX
14 July 2020